Miguel Bonnefoy was born in France in 1986 to a Venezuelan mother and a Chilean father. In 2013, he was awarded the prestigious Prix du jeune écrivain. His first novel, *Octavio's Journey*, was shortlisted for the Goncourt First Novel Award.

Emily Boyce is in-house translator and editor at Gallic Books.

Black Sugar

Black Sugar

Miguel Bonnefoy

Translated from the French by
Emily Boyce

Gallic Books

London

A Gallic Book
First published in France as *Sucre noir* by
Éditions Payot & Rivages, 2017
Copyright © Éditions Payot & Rivages, 2017

English translation copyright © Gallic Books, 2017
First published in Great Britain in 2017 by
Gallic Books, 59 Ebury Street,
London, SW1W 0NZ

A CIP record for this book is available from the British Library
ISBN 978-1-910477-52-6

Typeset in Fournier MT Pro by Gallic Books
Printed and bound by
CPI Group (UK) Ltd, Croydon, CR0 4YY
2 4 6 8 10 9 7 5 3 1

I

The dawn light revealed a ship marooned in the canopy of a vast forest. It was a square-rigged vessel with three masts and eighteen cannon, its stern wedged in the crown of a mango tree many metres tall. On the starboard side, fruits hung amid the rigging. To port, the hull was covered in thick undergrowth.

The ship had dried out, the only remaining trace of the sea a line of salt between the planks. There were no tides, no waves, only hills stretching as far as the eye could see. From time to time a breeze heavy with the scent of dried almonds blew in and the whole carcass of the ship from the topmast to the hold creaked like an old treasure chest being lowered into the ground.

For several days now, the crew had been struggling to survive. Aboard the ship were a motley group of non-commissioned officers, one-eyed bandits and black slaves with teeth cracked by rifle butts, who had been put in chains on the coast of Senegal and bought at a London market. For hours on end they stood at the ship's rail, their elbows resting on damp moss as they scoured the horizon for signs of the ocean.

Whole days went by with nothing to see but the green of the trees and birds flying out of the foliage.

Dressed in loincloths, the men came and went, wandering from one side of the ship to the other, stepping over the brambles that grew between the planks.

Some hung their hammocks high in order to avoid the climbing ivy. Others played dice, sitting on sacks of rubble. They no longer scrubbed the decks or cleared the hold. Only the first mate, a Haitian giant, cut a notch into the mast each day and listened out for sounds from a nearby port or the splash of an anchor amid the lapping of the forest's surf.

The frigate had sailed from Weymouth harbour several months earlier loaded with goods. It was built from mahogany, said to resist both rot and woodworm, and its sails had been coated in tar to withstand the wind. Just before its departure, a chaplain had conducted a service on the quayside and a shipwright had written the vessel's name on the bow for luck.

Sacks of lentils, beans and pulses were piled high in the 'tween decks; barrels of salted pork wrapped in strings of garlic stood next to a hundred pounds of honey from the viceroy of a distant province. The men had even brought a giant turtle on board and kept it alive on its back for weeks before cutting it open.

But the voyage was long. In the days following the shipwreck, biscuit and wine had to be rationed. Soon they could no longer rely on their provisions. The stifling heat had dried out the barrels, the pork joints rotted on the parapet and barely a drop of honey remained. When they ran out of lentils, they supped on herb soup from tin bowls. The biscuit turned to powder full of maggots to be gulped down with sawdust.

Warmed by the sun, the casks of water turned as black as a smithy's basin. The paintwork was flaking, rendering the ship's name illegible. The cannon turned into nests for birds of prey, the portholes becoming cages for bats. When at last the men went to eat the turtle, they lifted the shell to find no flesh left inside. All that remained were a few handfuls of red sand swirled into mysterious shapes – a black-magic alphabet according to a slave with knowledge of the occult.

The crew resolved to launch a land expedition to explore their surroundings. The first mate lowered himself on a chair attached to a rope and pulley. As he slid down, he made out the ship's belly through the gloom, its side gnawed away by moss. Fifty metres further down, a vast, sludgy, dark and swampy lagoon spread over hundreds of leagues into the heart of the forest.

The ground was muddy. The only trees were aquatic varieties whose roots were submerged. Intermingled tree trunks floated like rafts above the mangrove, woven with creepers and branches; channels wound beneath the arches of foliage and swallow carcasses lay suspended in the mud.

There was nothing of the ocean here. It was then that the first mate realised they were lost in the middle of a strange land where all the forces of nature appeared to stand in the way of their return to the sea.

Back on the deck, he said, 'The captain must be informed.'

Henry Morgan slept in a nook below deck which had no door, only a curtain strung across the entrance. The ship was under his orders, but he had not been seen outside his hideaway since the vessel had run aground.

The first mate lifted the curtain and entered the low-ceilinged room. In order to pass the threshold, he had to cut his way through with a machete. All kinds of tropical flowers were growing through the hatches. A thick layer of greenery had forced its way between the joists. Lemon-tree wardrobes were now wrapped in foliage and heavy furniture green with ferns creaked gently in the shadows.

The space was filled with curiosities from far-off places, spoils of plunder used as currency in foreign ports. Quintals of Moluccan cloves, Siamese ivory, Bengali cashmere and Timorese sandalwood were piled up on a table. The air carried the scent of Malabar pepper, kept fresh in a china pot.

On another table in the centre of the room, several coffers lay open, brimming with compasses and lizard-skin prayer books, with bottles of castor oil and Cayenne rum perched on top. Old nautical maps with Latin inscriptions, bound and gilded in Venice, were strewn about, and in the middle, set with strips of metal and twelve silver studs, stood an open oak chest that contained hundreds of écus, louis d'or, crosses and chalices, *morocotas*, several sabre handles, the neck of an Etruscan vase and the Golden Horns of Gallehus.

None but the first mate suspected that amid the stench of misery, hunger, rotten meat and inedible biscuit, a treasure trove languished beneath the muddy planks like an angel at the bottom of a pigsty.

The first mate spoke into the darkness.

'Captain, the men are growing restless.'

Something moved at the back of the room and, through the murk, a shape became visible on a four-poster bed.

The captain lay pale and thin, his head resting on nine pillows. He looked almost dead. He was staring at the branches coming in through the porthole. The smell of sickness hung in the air. Around him, the forest rumbled like a wave.

'Let them,' Henry Morgan replied hoarsely. 'It'll take their minds off their hunger.'

The first mate lit a candle, illuminating the captain's face with its French-style moustache, long hair caked with grease and hemp, and eyes bloodshot from forty years of piracy. The flame reddened his teeth and tinged his skin yellow. Mauve shadows gnawed away at his cheekbones.

He had the face of an old man, with deep wrinkles carved by his salt tan. Even in bed, he wore a grey leather coat with pistols tucked into the inside pockets and a tatty old tricorn hat with the look of something aged for twelve months in an oak barrel. Between his fingers he rolled hinged gold rings he had stolen in Barbados.

Henry Morgan leant over to the bedside table and poured himself a glass of rum with a squeeze of lime.

'If I had legs, I'd show them how a pirate survives,' he sniggered. 'Even on land.'

The captain lifted the sheet, revealing legs as fat as church bells with puffy, bluish, dropsy-ridden skin. Years of the bottle had put his veins under immense strain. The capillaries had leaked and the muscle tissue was swollen with fluid. His only relief came from pomegranate-bark infusions, vinegared pine broths and preparations of goat's milk mixed with ten ounces of cider.

The man who had been by turns privateer, commander in chief, brother of the coast and governor of Jamaica now slept for fourteen hours a day and pissed in his bed at night.

Shrivelled poultices lay beside bloodstained rags on the floor. An old slave put drains in his stomach and made ointments from aniseed and Mexican coriander, but Henry Morgan was dying in the depths of his ship, pitiful and alone, plunging his hands into treasure that could not save him.

'I'm not to be disturbed again,' he said.

He lay back down, adding, 'In a hanged man's home, there's no talk of ropes.'

*

The first mate saw immediately that the absence of a captain in a situation such as this could only end in mutiny. Yet hunger led the men not to revolt, but to hunt.

As if at sea, they strung fishing lines between hooks and hung nets on them to catch the birds which flew over the ship in their hundreds, like shoals of fish. But the traps yielded only tiny rodents, inedible iguanas and surprisingly cunning young monkeys, who escaped to steal the ship's tin plates. Lizards bit through the nets and bolted up the lines, slipping out of the sailors' grasp.

The first mate wove a basket of split reeds and creepers, placed a few pieces of fruit inside and attached it to a length of rope. Soon sharp tugs were felt. When the trap was opened, an animal emerged very slowly, setting its claws down on the planks.

It was a grey sloth, ugly as anything, with arms so long they doubled its overall size. It had no ears, eyes rimmed black as if with kohl, a squashed nose, flat face and thick fur. With slow, sad movements, it rocked its head from side to side as the crew crowded curiously around it.

'They're supposed to taste like lobster,' claimed the cook.

So they set up a brazier and barbecued the sloth to the sound of sea shanties. They served it with a few mangoes picked straight from the tree and a pair of fairly fleshy parrots caught in their migration south, marinated in lemon juice for two hours and cooked in banana leaves.

To save on salt, they used allspice. In place of crabs, they caught toads. And so this band of pirates used to feasting on piles of shrimp and shellfish, who had sailed the world many times but knew nothing of the fruits of the land, enjoyed their first and only rustic banquet aboard the ship.

A month later, the weather turned. The sky clouded over and a gale blew through the forest. Cold air was coming in from the sea. The frigate reeled and its stern rammed against the mango tree.

In the middle of the night, a powerful storm broke over the ship. The sails billowed. Leaves rained down, sailors were floored by falling branches and everyone clung to the parapet, tied to the rigging which was strained almost to breaking point. The frigate swayed in every direction, bobbing among the trees like a fishing float. Men were running, crawling, praying, barely able to stay upright on the slippery deck.

They battled the storm all night long. The keel moaned until dawn and one sailor took such fright that the very next day, out of patriotic superstition, he hoisted the national flag onto the jackstaff.

By morning, the hull was cracked and water was coming in from all sides. The wood was so rotten it smelt of old yeast. Though the ship had stopped swaying, the men still stood with their legs spread to keep their balance.

The first mate ordered an immediate inspection of the damage. From the keel to the top of the mast, six mariners compiled an inventory of every frayed rope, flattened screw and rusted nut. From high above, the lookout sent reports of sails and rope ladders torn down by the winds.

The first mate set a handful of the fittest sailors to tarring and caulking, sharing hammers, buckets of pitch and soaked oakum between them. Tied to one another with ropes, they had to saw up branches to replace planks, cut beams and secure the base of the mast. Heavy barrels were placed on the port side as counterweights. Hemp sheets were laid over the powder and when there was no tar left for sealing cracks, they resorted to mangrove sap.

The first mate summoned the men to the mess. He stood up solemnly to address the crew and said in a low voice, as if the devil were listening, 'Gentlemen, we are too heavy.'

Anything surplus to requirements was to be thrown overboard to lighten the load. They began with seven cannons and several kilos of lead used for smelting arms. Next they disposed of the fireboxes, grenades greased with lard, all the paraphernalia of war. Troughs of plants that had been growing in the hold were thrown into the abyss, and the last sulphur bombs were let off, scattering the vultures.

The ship went on creaking and sinking ever lower. The men were forced to throw out cabinets stolen during raids, globes all the way from Rome, and two large mirrors. It took several sailors to detach the chain from the anchor. Soon they were running in every direction, silhouettes spooked by the ship's groans, arms full of provisions and pine chests, rolling leaky barrels along the deck.

Coffee and dried fruits were carried off, but the first mate forbade anyone to touch the spices, because in Europe a peppercorn was worth more than a man's life.

The forest was covered in goods, silks and pillaged paintings. A sail came loose, landing bonnet-like on distant treetops. Feathered hats, velvet breeches and ladies' undergarments hung from the branches. Fragments of the ship, topsails and oars were discarded, while barrels of Madeira wine were brought up on deck to be drunk in haste.

Birds clutched copper and silver bracelets in their beaks. Marquises' dresses floated in the breeze above the canopy and monkeys played with pieces of lace, jumping from tree to tree, tearing up the pirates' black flag.

Yet still the frigate remained too heavy and still it sank deeper. The men were losing patience. The first mate drew aside the curtain of the captain's nook, with two sailors following behind.

Henry Morgan was alone, lying on the bed in his hideout. By the light of a candle, he was counting his gold coins before an open chest. When he saw that the men were armed, he quickly sat up and reached for his pistol.

'Captain, we must clear this room,' said the first mate.

Henry Morgan aimed his gun at the doorway. His face, ravaged by alcohol, had turned deathly pale. The weapon shook in his hand.

'No,' he replied. 'First we must clear the ship.'

He opened fire and one of the sailors fell. The men took out their sabres and a furious battle broke out on deck.

As each man fell, his body was thrown overboard. Henry Morgan yelled, shooting into the crowd and promising a share of the booty to all those who would protect him. A circle formed around him.

There was fierce fighting in a jumble of shots and black sabre clashes; some used rusty scythes or wooden legs. All were fighting, the seaman to defend his freedom, the slave to gain his, and as the brawl went on the boat pitched in the canopy.

The skirmish lasted two hours. There were thirty dead, eleven deserters, and the cook was found stabbed in the fork of a tree. By the end, only the captain, ten men who had protected him and the gravely injured first mate remained.

Henry Morgan lay on his bed, delirious with exhaustion. The ground was littered with rubbish, severed fingers and broken pots. Several bodies had not been recovered. The captain knew he could not tolerate a mutiny under his leadership and since he had the right by royal decree to put crew members to death, he was determined to make an example of one of the culprits.

The first mate was shivering in the corner,

clutching his side to stem the flow of blood. Without further ado, the captain ordered that he be tried for sedition. To assert his authority, he wished to follow the procedure of the English courts, invoking divine justice and the tradition of the worst executions at the Tower of London.

On deck, a pirate was dressed as a clerk and the wounded were called as witnesses. The sole crew member able to read and write was asked to record the proceedings. A one-armed man overseeing the trial rushed through the hearing and pronounced the verdict at midday. Henry Morgan donned a judge's wig and signed the ruling himself, punishing a crime by committing another.

Half an hour later, in this remote land in the middle of a rainforest, the barbaric punishments of the European courts were carried out thousands of miles away in the green light of the almond trees, as the first mate was beheaded with an axe.

Henry Morgan was becoming a legend and losing his mind. He demanded to be taken on deck to watch the head roll. Four men were lifting the bed onto their shoulders when suddenly a load crack was heard nearby, as if a huge chunk of the ship had broken free. A dull thud followed and the floor beneath them began to rock from side to side. Henry Morgan had to cling to the bedpost to avoid falling out.

At that moment, a sailor came in, buffeted by the ship's seesawing motion.

'Captain, the keel's just snapped.'

He added, 'The stem is torn and the hull is split. The ship is crumbling like a sugar lump. The rain will soon be upon us,' he went on breathlessly. 'The ship cannot withstand another storm.'

All around, planks were snapping. The trees could no longer support the hull. Standing near the bed, the sailor took a look at the chest Henry Morgan was clutching in his arms.

'Captain, gold is heavy. Allow me to help.'

As he held out his hand, Henry Morgan spat globules of blood in his face. His mouth was twisted in a wicked cackle.

'I'm taking it with me,' he said. 'Death must come at a price.'

The weight of the boat uprooted the trees and dragged the ship down into the abyss. A cloud of dust rose and filled the sky. Animals took fright at the commotion. And so it was that Henry Morgan's frigate was so entirely consumed by nature's passionate, swampy depths that no trace of it was ever found, and the treasure lay buried amid scraps of sail and a pirate's corpse, preserved within the belly of the Caribbean.

II

Three centuries later a village was built where the boat had disappeared. At that time it was no more than a small, remote community at the edge of a forest, living off what it produced. Milk was delivered to people's homes, ice was a luxury and villagers set their watches by the flight of the birds.

The women carried baskets of fruit on their heads to a nameless, statueless square along streets which were not yet paved, the paths dusty in the dry season and muddy when the rains came. Before a line of trees, a valley opened up, striped with fields of sunflowers whose long leaves bent with the breeze. In the distance stood the ruins of a chapel where an English pirate ship was said to have gone aground.

A man passing through the village had once attested to the legend of Captain Henry Morgan's lost treasures, having heard the story from missionaries who had found coins of untold value in the marshes. Although the news spread quickly, the countryside was not suddenly overrun by bearded, chattering gold-diggers with spades slung over their shoulders and sieves in their hands.

The peasants in this quiet backwater could not read

a map or calculate a meridian, they could only work a sickle, grow maize and grind it by hand. Since there was nothing to buy and everything to build, gold was worth less than iron. They knew nothing of pirates and most had never seen the sea.

No longer a tribe, nor yet a people, they were born into a static existence governed by the slow pace of the harvests and died leaving flimsy structures in the valley behind them.

The poorest dwellings in the west had gardens enclosed only by natural barriers, surrounded by guava fields from which floral scents drifted for leagues on inland breezes. In the east, fine planters' residences had been built in colonial style with pitched roofs, bronze gates and balustraded balconies that looked out over the plantations.

In between, coffee, bananas and sugar cane were grown on small farms on a quiet plain at the edge of the forest.

The Otero family's farm was white-walled with ruby-red roof tiles and had been built to face the sun. The front door, with its knocker shaped like an open hand in welcome, led into a large living and dining area furnished with monastic simplicity.

Freshly picked flowers spilt from terracotta vases and every room had a window looking out on the road or the gardenia-filled back yard. Here stood brick ovens and, at the back, a large outbuilding constructed for the breeding of fighting cocks but which now housed only a handful of sickly hens.

The Oteros had bought the property for a song, when the land, neglected for decades, had plummeted in value and had had to be put up for sale.

Though the facade with its dilapidated shutters was ugly, inside the building was filled with a pleasant mixture of sugary and woody scents. The whole house, from the hallway up to the top floor, was bathed in a warm light the colour of leather or aged oak. In the morning, wild winds brought in an ash-coloured dust laden with cicadas and omens. Come nightfall, everything had a purplish tinge.

There were three bedrooms upstairs with yellowed walls, and a separate small room on the ground floor, furnished haphazardly with three rush chairs, a bed and muslin curtains.

This room had never been occupied. The house had been sold on condition that the back room remain untouched. The clause had no legal standing but each of the house's owners felt morally obliged to abide by it, to the extent that neither the Oteros nor, later, the Bracamontes ever set foot in the dark room whose door was opened only once a year.

Religiously every 1 November, an old woman would enter the house carrying an empty bucket, walk straight to the room and shut herself inside for hours. The former owner of the house, she came to mourn her late husband.

She would fill her bucket with tears, light seven candles with buttered wicks and drink cinnamon wine. Stooped, her head covered with a mourning mantilla, wearing a tattered lace dress, she looked up only in order to talk to God. Her leathery skin seemed to have been smoked dry. Across her brow lay a lock of grey hair, yellowed with time like a strip of corn.

She emerged again in the middle of the night, turning the key several times in the door behind her, crossing the living room and, as she passed through the porch, would murmur to Señor Otero: 'See you next year, Señor.'

He never replied. He stayed up late into the night, rocking in his rattan chair, smoking his pipe and gazing out at his plantations.

Ezequiel Otero was a man of simple habits, with no taste for travel or ostentation. He had a wide forehead, a low nose and bushy eyebrows. He had grown up in this region abandoned to the sun, as part of a humble Christian family, his father a farmer before him.

Since childhood, he had trodden the same path behind the plough day after day, cutting sugar cane without thinking and pressing it with his bare arms. His thin, hairy body was bowed by fatigue and hazy desires, beaten down by farm work and the uncertainties of harvests. He wore a suit made of a light beige-coloured fabric, hemp espadrilles and a machete strapped across his chest.

His wife, Candelaria de Otero, née Castillo, was always very modestly dressed, with cotton dresses buttoned up to her chin and starched ecru collars. She kept a little ivory cross tucked inside the sleeve of her cardigan and walked like the sisters who once trod the corridors of lazarettos with their veils, headbands and tightly pinned wimples.

She loved to be complimented on the fine condition of her crockery, her choice of furniture and her husband's good health. Her sheets were scented with flowers tucked between their folds. She was a woman of steadfast patience and to the end of her days stood at the stove preparing Creole soups, gazing into the pan in a kitchen where hams hung from the ceiling.

The only child of this unremarkable couple was a girl named Serena Otero. They had had her so late in life that the mother had long since given up the idea of becoming pregnant, the father that of another mouth to feed. And so the child was born into a home for the elderly, filled with outdated objects and old furniture and inhabited by a couple drained of all strength and enthusiasm, tired of living.

Serena's solitary existence led her to withdraw into herself. She had no playmates, never rolled in the grass, escaped the bumps and scrapes of childhood and spoke very polished, proper Spanish with a slight provincial lilt. She became accustomed to saying very little, making few gestures, and living lazily.

For hours at a time, she would squat in her bedroom, looking out of the window at the flowers in the meadow or patiently awaiting the evening rosary. Afraid of the dark, before bed she would fill her bedside lamps with corozo oil and slide under her tulle mosquito net to go to sleep.

Serena Otero spent so much time observing the

landscape that she developed an interest in botany and a talent for drawing flowers. In the forest she picked lobster-claw and bird-of-paradise plants, West Indian jasmine and porcelain roses, and collected herbariums. She carried under her arm a sketchbook she had bound from textured paper and sticks of charcoal that blackened her pockets.

Before lunchtime, she would tramp through the undergrowth in her brightly coloured skirts, holding a little metal shovel and a black embroidered basket. Though at first glance her arms appeared weak, when she pulled up a root or hauled cratefuls of dirt, her taut, rounded, robust muscles, youthful suppleness and sturdy nature were clear to see.

Tall and light on her feet, she did not look like her fellow country-women. Her hair was lighter than most, she had a sensual mouth and was so slender that even the most stubborn-hearted could not but be moved at the sight of her. A whole court of young admirers soon flocked to her, but Serena Otero was bored by their advances and kept dreaming of new horizons until the day she died.

In the evenings she sat hunched at the table with her hair tied back, barely touching her plate or saying a word as she watched her soup go cold. She would pick up a red-footed tortoise twenty years her senior, put it on her lap and stroke it gently, her head bowed.

Talk at the dinner table revolved around the usual worries about the house or the mill, the thickness of the molasses and the arrival of the dry season. It had been the same for the past sixteen years. First the father and then the mother recounted the events of their day while Serena remained a stranger to her own family, enduring these interminable meals and watching the dishes pass before her with neither relish nor revulsion.

Only one thing could shake her out of her torpor. Across the room, beside the window, she had installed a wireless with numerous buttons and nickel levers. This was a fairly recent invention, and probably the most modern thing in the entire village.

The wireless set had a battery, various reels, a long antenna and a speaker shaped like the neck of a swan. It was rectangular with black ebonite marquetry motifs, and emitted a series of whistling, whining and crackling sounds. They turned it on after supper and, as the father smoked his pipe and the mother sat knitting, the distant voice of a radio presenter emerged from the bowels of the device.

Serena soaked up every word the man said. Around eight o'clock, after the news bulletin, the old waltzes and the cooking programmes, a daily slot was dedicated to listeners in the village, read by a wise and soothing voice. In the absence of a postal service, the station transmitted personal messages, the presenter reading out clumsily handwritten notes from one farmer to another.

This allowed them to learn the names of their neighbours and hear reports of births, deaths, forthcoming marriages, and disputed inheritances.

People bartered the price of cattle, informed each other of slaughter times and, each new season with naïve enthusiasm, announced the arrival of the merchant caravans.

It was around this time that a medium placed an advertisement on the radio: 'Dr Esmeralda Cadenas, professional medium, communicates with all ranks of the departed and secures exclusive visits from the other side. Ten minutes, ten pesos. Intimate encounters, twenty pesos.'

Esmeralda Cadenas made a name for herself the day a dead person replied to her advertisement. He claimed to be a local naval cadet who had drowned eight years earlier in a navigation accident during an expedition. Everyone took this to be a prank, until the phenomenon was repeated. After that, no one questioned this public exchange of letters which defied the fundamental laws of biology, but followed the nightly instalments like a soap opera.

A fashion for spiritualism began. Charlatans sprang up and table-turning sessions were organised. But a few weeks later it came to light that the author of the replies was not a drowned young naval cadet, but the radio presenter himself, who had been struck by Dr Esmeralda Cadenas's imaginative daring and had put on the voice of the departed in an attempt to please her.

Serena Otero had followed the story with fascination. In an effort to combat the boredom of her daily life, she thought of sending her own messages to a mystery recipient. Though the man she wrote to did not exist, she trusted she could make him appear on the strength of her words alone.

As the month of November wore on, she took up the pseudonym Maria Dolores and spent several days composing her first announcement to the radio station. Lyrical, filled with crossings-out, it received no reply.

The following week, she wrote another, more emotionally charged version, followed by a third and, within five weeks, Serena Otero had sent fifty impassioned messages in which she offered the depths of her soul to a man who was probably yet to be born.

When still nothing had been aired, she decided to cut it down to two sentences:

Maria Dolores hereby announces that she has drowned her heart in a barrel of rum. Reward offered to whoever comes to drink it.

The first time the presenter read out her announcement, the family was eating in the front room. Serena was so moved at the sound of her words coming out of the wireless, she was convinced the man would appear that very evening. But her face gave nothing away, not the tiniest flicker of emotion.

Protected by the anonymity of her pseudonym, Serena gave her parents no reason to suspect her dual identity. She did her best to avoid attracting attention, maintaining her usual cold stare, but inside her youthful form she tasted that powerful, hidden, unspoken joy that is the preserve of adolescents discovering how it feels to love.

From then on, she wrote new announcements every day, varying the phrasing, creating a coded language between herself and the outside world. Though she never received any replies, she found herself blissfully happy, emboldened and serene in their absence. She succumbed less often to boredom, obsessively counting down the hours until evening came.

At dinner, she ate with more appetite. When her father told them about his day, she cut him off to tell him about her own. She marvelled at perfectly ordinary things and even made small talk. A self-centred only child, she barely stopped to think that this sudden change of humour might arouse suspicion.

When they finished eating, she was the first to stand up from the table to turn the radio on. Sitting by the window, watching her reflection in the glass, she heard the presenter read out the announcement addressed to no one but herself and, before the mirror of the night sky, dreamed of a man in her own image.

After a few months, the fantasy of a handsome stranger one day sitting at her table became a matter of absolute certainty.

Serena imagined him to be tall, broad-necked, and with a kind face. Ready to submit to this phantom man's every desire, she came up with an infinite number of poetic names for him, and pictured him clasping her forcefully to his chest, both of them giving themselves up to a primal act.

In herbal notebooks smelling of musk and lavender, her adolescent hand recorded this torrent of passion, devotion and overwhelming sensations, and the words flowed from the anonymity of her bedroom to all the radios of the valley, ringing out like a desperate appeal.

One night, as the rainy season was drawing to a close, they heard footsteps outside the house. Serena felt her heart pounding against her chest. Her father went to open the door and returned alone, but behind him in the doorway the figure of the house's former owner suddenly appeared, moving falteringly in her black lace, heaving her aged legs towards the back room.

It was 1 November. A year had gone by since the first announcement. Serena felt a pang of pain. She brought the tortoise to her lap and sat hunched over the table until nine o'clock, stroking the cold carapace over and over again, her bored, abandoned heart retreating into a shell of its own.

III

During the second week of December, a figure no one recognised entered the village, speaking with an accent from the other side of the country.

The man came bearing the sounds and noises of the city, its factory smog and feverish modernity. He wore an impeccably stylish white linen suit, boots which buttoned up to the ankle and a rather elegant rectangular poncho, knotted at the shoulder, with his name embroidered on it in silver thread.

His name was Severo Bracamonte, for at this time, not long after colonial rule, people went by the names of former governors. He had arrived by the road that led to the main farm buildings, following a row of guava trees.

He was a young man in his twenties with delicate skin and a fragile frame. The son of a white man and an indigenous woman, he was smooth-faced with a narrow brow framed by black hair, and when he frowned, his pale eyes gave him the stern yet innocent look of a young traveller of the world.

The first building he came to was the sugar mill. Round the back, Señor Otero was loading sugar cane into a wheelbarrow. Severo Bracamonte offered to help in exchange for a glass of rum. He took off his poncho, hung it on a branch and got to work.

It was the time of day when there were no shadows, the heat was intense and the sun burnt into their necks, but the two men carried on regardless, moving the sugar cane for several hours more, exchanging simple words, speeding up their pace to make the most of the daylight.

Night began to fall. They sat down in the shade of a low wall. Otero poured his visitor a glass of rum and, by sharing a drink, a sense of mutual respect began to grow between them, like friends breaking bread. They talked about crushing the stems to make tafia, about the mill built on top of a chessboard of bamboo, and the height of the palms planted in the field below them.

The two men poured themselves another glass and talked and drank as if they had long been bound by their shared labours – as if work had made brothers of them.

The clock struck eight. Otero asked the young man to dinner with his wife and daughter. They hung a lamp from the ceiling beam in the dining room. Candelaria Otero cut off a hen's head ready to stew it, and cooked pork kebabs over a wood fire. They huddled around the table.

Noticing Serena's empty seat, her mother called her several times to no avail, and said calmly, 'Our daughter won't be long.'

But Serena was already standing stock-still in the doorway, staring at the dinner guest.

Severo Bracamonte looked nothing like the man she had imagined. His thin neck, unfinished shoulders and colourless lips gave him the appearance of a wounded animal. She was reluctant to look closely at this puny, almost feminine body, a form both strangely graceful and uncommonly feeble. His face was covered in brown, grainy freckles and his eyes, with their long, black lashes, were dark-circled, dull and clouded like moiré silk.

She saw at once that the world had heard her cries and mocked them. Severo Bracamonte was ugly. Try as she might to find some hidden beauty, a spark of intelligence or glimmer of mischief in the lines of his face, she had now to accept the fact that fate had set out to try her, and that she would need to draw on all her reserves of courage and charity if ever she was to love this man.

The stranger had taken off his poncho and left his belongings by the door. Resting his elbow on the table, he looked around at the old furniture. The soup was served. As the family was not used to having guests, nobody spoke. A chill descended.

Severo understood. In an effort to please his hosts, he told stories of adventurers and pirates. He made easy conversation and was quick off the mark. He chose his words carefully, holding back where necessary, and spoke in a voice full of flourish.

He had a brother who was the foreman in charge of the restoration of a church in San Pablo del Limón. No sooner had he mentioned this than Otero asked for news of the capital, in which he had not set foot for thirty years.

'Thirty years?' Severo replied, surprised. 'Times have changed, Señor Otero. Picture this, they've appointed a black bishop. They've built a tramline. But everything's so expensive.'

'Oh, isn't it everywhere!' Ezequiel Otero cried.

'I had to seek my fortune elsewhere,' Severo went on. 'I've come a long way, if only you knew ... the soles of my shoes are worn out and my purse is empty. But a long time ago in a far-off port, my eyes turned yellow at the sight of my first gold nugget.'

'You've gold?' Otero asked, amazed.

Severo Bracamonte told him no, he was not carrying any gold, only a few small pieces of amber given to him by a merchant from the Baltic. Receiving this present had been like finding a precious stone in the mud.

'The advantage of being poor,' he smiled, 'is you can only get richer.'

He took from his bag a series of ropes, an old map that was falling to pieces, and a little tin box, which he opened. It was filled with little musk-scented amber stones the colour of honey.

'In daylight, they shine like gold,' he said wisely. 'But here, look what the merchant sold me.'

He rummaged in his bag once more and pulled out a wodge of papers which he placed on the table. These, he explained, were twenty pages of documents, old letters and muddled correspondence on the subject of a stash of buried treasure. There were copies of records and a number of quill-pen sketches he said had been drawn by members of foreign expeditions.

He went on: 'All the information on Captain Henry Morgan's lost treasure is here, down to its precise location. There's no legend without proof. I must admit, Señor Otero ... I can't wait to start digging, exploring the region and studying my maps.'

Without waiting for the family to react, Severo Bracamonte told them he wished to propose a deal: if the Oteros let him stay with them, he would give them a share of the booty.

He told them he would not take advantage of their hospitality, would sleep at a respectful distance from the family and eat only a little. He opened his eyes wide, put his hand on his heart and assured them they need only look him in the eye to see he was an honest soul.

Ezequiel Otero was taken aback by the sudden turn the conversation had taken.

'Why would a pirate hide his treasure this far from the sea?' he asked innocently.

Severo Bracamonte pointed at the uncultivated land outside the window and replied, as if it were perfectly obvious: 'Because people bury treasure in land that will never change.'

Ever more astonished, Otero asked him what the treasure consisted of. At that point, Severo put down his knife and fork, wiped his mouth on his napkin and pushed his chair back to give himself space.

'I'm talking about thousands of Roman coins and emeralds the size of fists. I'm talking about the Flota de Oro and church chalices from Lima. I'm talking about a solid-gold statue of the Virgin two metres tall with seven diamond crowns. I'm talking about ...'

His voice was choked with emotion and his cheeks burnt bright red. He finished his sentence with a sweeping, extravagant gesture, throwing his arms wide, and all eyes were on him. Serena Otero had said nothing.

She had listened to his tales without touching her plate or batting an eyelid. Her hands were firmly clasped together beneath the table and she stared straight at Severo Bracamonte at the other end of the table.

In the space of a few minutes, he had painted a damning portrait that told you all you needed to know about him. This was not the handsome stranger who had heard her letters to the radio station, but a man of avaricious, greedy appetites, a pleasure-seeker who lived by his luck, indiscriminately driven by his own passions. He didn't want to be loved; he wanted to be rich.

Serena felt choked and crumpled. Her face flushed with anger. She would have grabbed him by the throat had her good manners not held her back. In an attempt to calm her feverish nerves, she stood up and went to open the window. The air stank of manure.

Back at the table, she did her best to look calm and normal, even forcing herself to compliment her mother on the soup. Beside her, Candelaria Otero ate silently, and came and went, leaving only the vague scent of raisins in her path.

Serena's father seemed amused by Severo's proposition, saying, 'Why not?' and looking quite plainly at Severo while slapping him good-naturedly on the back.

Pleased at the prospect of a deal that cost him nothing, Ezequiel Otero turned to Serena to ask if she could see any reason why this 'talented' gold-digger shouldn't stay a few days.

Serena leapt to her feet and, before leaving the room, said bluntly and without betraying a hint of surprise, 'It takes more than talent to find treasure, Father.'

IV

The Oteros allowed Severo Bracamonte to sleep in the shed in the back yard. It had a pitched roof and a single window whose light was partially blocked by a trellis of flowers. Inside, an old claw-foot bathtub had been piled with sacks of sand, broken tools, doorknobs and bird perches.

The room smelt of ammonia and chicken coops. A petrol lamp hanging from a wire strung loosely between two rods planted in the ground cast its light over a chair and a bed.

Once he had settled in, Severo Bracamonte began to pin articles on prospecting companies, maps of mines and pictures of gold panners on a noticeboard. He had spent his youth collecting anything he could find on the subject of buried treasure: images of past expeditions, historical accounts, scraps of parchment, planispheres and even a ship's log written in a surgeon-pirate's left hand, containing what may well have been coded plans for a hiding place.

This was how Severo spent his first month shut inside his refuge. Like an alchemist at his stove, he did not wish to be disturbed.

He studied the adventures of the Spanish, who

had launched expeditions in search of a kingdom of gold, cloves and cinnamon, and dreamed of animals feeding on opals and rubies. He believed in Walter Raleigh's Guiana, the precious stones in the sands of the Yuruarí river and the founding of San Francisco.

As he quietly set about his quest, he celebrated the memory of all the men who had gone before him, trudging through the river silt, wading through the inland bogs, empty-bellied, cutting the soles of their feet on the diamonds.

Before heading out, he divided the search area into zones and scouted out underground tunnels. In order to waste as little exploration time as possible, he spent many hours checking the accuracy of his set of compasses.

Alone in his shed, he spent whole days studying old maps of islands, cursing their imprecise angles and scales and, despite a lack of scientific knowledge, came up with equations more accurate than the cartographers'.

After a month he headed out into the undergrowth, his bag heavy with provisions—a tin coffee pot, cassava pancakes and a bag of tapioca flour. He held a metal rod in one hand for testing the rivers he crossed; in the other, a saddlebag filled with candles, a knife and measuring instruments, and he had a heavy wooden shovel over his right shoulder.

Each time he reached a clearing, he would inspect his surroundings and make drawings. He carefully noted every area he had explored on a map, adding all the important landmarks to ensure he didn't return to the same spot twice. In place of a compass he used a little magnetic dial bought at a market which showed the direction of the sea.

During the day, he tapped the earth, his ear to the ground, trying to hear the echo of an underground hollow. At night, he followed the stars across the sky and thought he saw treasure when will-o'-the-wisps danced above the caves.

He soon learnt to recognise the sturdiest branches and would throw mud-caked ropes around them to string up his hammock. As he roamed, he found plenty of fresh water for his flask, along with logs for his fire washed up on the riverbanks.

He had read so much about pirates that he knew how to build a buccan and grill meat in the smoke. He washed in streams, slept on stony ground and ate dry bread, living like a convict but never losing heart, for all that his fortune remained as elusive as ever.

But the weeks went by and still he found nothing. The reward for his months of work was long in coming. On weary nights when he felt his strength draining away from him, he became his own worst enemy, staring at the horizon as a condemned man contemplates the noose. He was all dejection and fatigue, which combined in him like jumbled coins in a treasure chest, and he returned to the shed empty-handed, with brambles in his hair, breathing iguana breath.

*

When not out exploring, Severo Bracamonte drew respectfully on the Oteros' hospitality. At around eight in the morning, he would help the mother to water the herbs, and at around eight in the evening, he would sit on the porch smoking a pipe with the father as the shadows turned blue.

The family were aware he was a long way from home, that he wasn't eating properly and was sleeping in a henhouse, so they always left a little warm soup for him at their table.

None of them complained about their guest – none but Serena Otero. Severo's presence annoyed her. She addressed him formally, was cool and distant with him, and never had a kind word to say to him. Severo, on the other hand, was always talkative, and at dinner would often joke about his own ignorance of farming matters. Serena remained unmoved, her lips clamped shut. Over the course of the meal, in the lamplight, a chasm opened up between them.

She blamed him for not being the one she had been waiting for. She had dreamed of an illusion, an object of desire, and he was just a man. A year ago she would have laughed if someone had told her that her mysterious stranger would come in search not of love, but gold.

If she now seemed pinched, sour and serious, it was not a mark of indifference on her part, but a sign that Severo had come to dominate her thoughts to the point of obsession. He made her uncomfortable, flooding her mind with doubts the moment he entered the dining room. She allowed her head to fill with a thousand questions, risky responses and conflicting emotions and, despite her best efforts, the slight figure of the gold-digger loomed large, disrupting the unchanging order of her days.

In October, she lost patience. After all these months he had still found no treasure and she announced to her father that if Severo continued to return empty-handed, they ought to think about sending him away.

One tense evening at the dinner table she fixed his leaving date herself, her parents agreed, and before he went to sleep in his shed that night, Severo Bracamonte prayed that God might come to him in his dreams with a gold coin and save him.

The next day at the first light of dawn, he picked up a spade, wrapped a rope around his chest and headed down the slope towards the river. He walked for two hours into the heart of the forest, skirting a valley carved out of limestone bedrock which rose to bright white heights.

At the foot of a hill he came across the entrance to a cave, blocked by rocks and a tangle of brambles. Severo fought his way inside, but as he entered the gloom, he realised that the earth beneath his feet had been carved up – a telltale sign that other gold-diggers had been here before him. After another few steps, he made out footprints in the mud. He began to dig, having calculated that this was a good place to look, and the sound of his pickaxe echoed like a voice in the cavern's throat.

He was still digging when something hard in the ground stopped him mid-swing.

Severo stepped up his efforts and suddenly a patch of white skin appeared at his feet. He swept away the layer of earth covering his find and saw emerging before him what appeared to be a woman's breast.

Severo threw himself to his knees and began digging with his bare hands, throwing the earth between his legs like a crazed dog. After half an hour the body of a woman seven feet tall appeared out of the muck, lying at the bottom of a cave like a drowned woman languishing at the bottom of a lake.

Severo made the sign of the cross. He set to work brushing her clean and scooping out the earth around her. When he finally managed to haul her up, first with his arms and then levering her with his pickaxe, he saw it was a Roman statue of Diana the Hunter delicately carved out of Italian marble; it had lain here for centuries.

The statue had a refined hairstyle for the times, with two locks of hair falling over her brow, an elegant figure and breasts that sat high on her chest. Her head was tilted to one side with an air of chaste nostalgia and her feet were entwined with an arabesque of vine leaves. Her tunic, whose folds had emerged unscathed, was hitched up to the knees, the better to run in, and in her closed left fist she held a bow, half of which had been lost so that it now resembled a buffalo horn.

The statue bore the marks of its years underground. Around the neck there were deep cracks, mud stains and the white of the marble had dulled. The right hand was fingerless and the nose split.

Yet its face expressed not indifference or sternness at the neglect it had suffered, but goodwill and cordiality, a humanity close to nature perhaps only because it had endured the chill and solitude below ground for so long.

That night Severo returned to the house pulling the statue behind him with a ship's rope slung over his shoulder, and stood it beside the front door.

Señor Otero came outside, clutching his head in his hands, fascinated by Severo's discovery, convinced he was in the presence of a divine apparition. He launched into a rendition of the hymn 'Ave Maris Stella', joined by his wife, whose eyes shone as if before the Virgin Mary. Faced with this gift from the heavens, she wanted to cut off her hair with silver scissors that very night and cover the statue's head with it, but Severo reminded her that classical mythology had nothing to do with the Bible.

Feeling proud of himself, he told them that this was only the first of the offerings he would give in exchange for their hospitality, that there would be many more to come – the region being full of surprises – and concluded, with the certainty of those whom nature rewards: 'Every statue is known to have its treasure.'

V

For fifty years, the marble statue stood outside the entrance to the house, exposed to the tropical rains and humidity, staring into the void in the mysterious way of things found without being sought.

Severo Bracamonte was more convinced than ever that his happiness lay two metres below ground in a chest sealed by twelve four-inch studs. The Sunday after his discovery of the statue, in the courtyard behind the church in which he had not wished to pray, he thanked God, while the Otero family took the sacrament beneath imitation gold vaults.

He felt nothing could sway him from his sublime mission, and even the failures of his predecessors, who had left this earth as poor as they had entered it, served only to feed his determination.

He understood that to be a successful gold-digger required not only daring but careful calculation, the plodding routine work of collecting shared knowledge and making enquiries. He began asking the locals questions, trying to sort historical fact from popular wisdom.

He knocked at every door, sat at every table. No sooner had he been given some clue than he would start investigating it. It was all part of the story. Indefatigable, his eyes bright with curiosity, he would gather testimony, remember the names of shepherds, link memories and compare letters. People allowed him into their homes, giving him access to family documents and letting him open up old registers and yellowed albums.

So through a mixture of rigour and effervescence, enthusiasm and patience, faith and reason, he eventually met all the villagers and made a name for himself.

One night, Severo Bracamonte heard on the wireless that an English engineer had invented an instrument for locating metals buried underground. It had been used to detect landmines after the First World War and to find bullets lodged in soldiers' bodies.

Severo bought a shiny new metal detector by mail order from the capital. The modern appliance arrived in the archaic landscape in the bottom of a pirogue and was unloaded at the landing stage on the river where fabulous caged birds were sold. On its way to its new home, the detector had come through stilted villages and passed children bathing noisily in rivers, and had travelled by cattle truck for several days, dodging the customs posts, skirting banana plantations and parrot farms.

The metal detector weighed almost fifteen kilos. Equipped with dry-cell batteries and an old headset, it took both hands to lift it. When it came across a metal object, it made a weak sound which grew louder as it got closer, and in the first few days Severo was easily able to dig up a number of thimbles, lead medals and a stop-tap key.

The effectiveness of this sophisticated device was hindered by greasy soil and dense undergrowth. But Severo kept going, staying out until midnight, covering dozens of kilometres, drunk on hope and good fortune, confident of achieving miraculous results in the name of progress.

Taking advantage of his absence one day, Serena went outside to look at the statue of Diana. Though she took care not to let it show, she fell under the spell of the marble woman watching over the entrance to the house. She examined each of her fractures in detail, studied the lovely grain of her skin and ran her hands over the drape of her tunic. The statue's strong pose brought to mind all the dignified, powerful, regal women who had stood tall throughout the centuries, and whose voices carried beyond their deep resting places. For the first time, she thought of Severo without animosity or pride, and told herself with a mixture of admiration and detachment that only a poet could bring such a marvel as this Diana back to life.

For she knew as well as he what traps the forest laid. She knew how reluctant the earth was to part with its riches. She spent her time scouring the woods in search of wonders of the organic kind, and pursued her treasure hunt just as doggedly as Severo Bracamonte did his.

Every morning she set out across the fields armed with a shovel and a pruning knife, cutting bulbs and pressing leaves between her fingers as she went. A dedicated herbalist, she loaded up her saddlebag with a watering can, three small plant boxes, twenty sheets of paper and a pine board and headed for the clearings where peonies, camellias, cactuses and heliotropes flowered.

She sketched cocoplums and soursop pips. Whenever she found a patch of shade, she would sit cross-legged, open her notebook and classify her findings in an order only she understood. She stuck labels next to each drawing with invented scholarly names, the date and place of collection, the length of the stalk and exact colour of the flower, renaming a natural world that predated her by millions of years.

At dusk, she rushed back to her room, buzzing like a bee, spreading out and pressing the leaves she had collected. To keep seedlings alive, she mixed them with manure and slid them into vials sealed with mastic. She bagged up seeds, potted young plants and then, by the light of a candle, made crayon sketches enhanced with gouache paints.

There, surrounded by her herb collections, amid the names of all the plants, she felt herself dissolving like sugar in water, melding with everything around her, absorbed in the long and serene osmosis of writing.

One evening, Severo Bracamonte saw Serena walking close to his shed. He wondered if this unusual occurrence might signal a secret wish for friendship, and the thought lit up his heart in a way he had never imagined.

Bolstered by his discovery of the statue, without fear of rejection, he went out to speak to her.

'I know science and you know the land. Let's help one another.'

Serena looked back at him in amusement and replied evenly, 'You don't know science.'

Severo didn't contradict her. 'But you do know the land.'

He invited her in, but she refused. So he asked her to wait outside while he went to look for something, emerging carrying a cardboard box.

To house Serena's plants and flowers, Severo had made two boxes out of wood and glass, with a protective brass grille to keep the earth damp through condensation.

'See,' he said. 'I do know science.'

He invited her in once again and this time she agreed, but said she would only stay a minute.

The shed was poorly lit. A map of the region was stuck on the wall, covered in arrows, numbers and incomprehensible symbols. Serena asked what it all meant.

'This is what will lead me to the treasure,' explained Severo, pleased to have made an impression.

He smiled, betraying his satisfaction and a glimmer of mischief. He sat down opposite her and tried his best to sound interesting.

'See that red circle? That's your house. The green spaces? That's the forest. The blue line? The river. The rest – the marks, dots, flags and all that – those are possible locations for the treasure.'

Serena brought her face close to the wall to try to make sense of the map. She saw straight away that this depiction of the forest bore no relation to her own impression of it. There were no flowers marked on it, the colours did not correspond to those she had grown up looking at, and the river, roughly drawn in the wrong shade of blue, went too far into the plains.

'Where did you find the statue?'

Severo placed his finger on a red star between the river and the edge of the forest. Serena looked closer, took measurements with her thumb and index finger, spent a long time staring at the map and finally declared, 'In that case you walked straight past the treasure without noticing it.'

Severo stiffened, staring at her. Serena laughed. She took a perverse pleasure in having regained the conversational upper hand with just a few words.

Since he remained frozen, she stood up, filled briefly with confidence and some childish feeling, and shook him.

'Follow me,' she said.

She left the shed and led the way into the forest, striding ahead of him.

They followed a path she seemed to know well. It was getting dark already. They walked quickly towards the river, stomping through piles of sticky, mud-covered leaves, delving into the undergrowth. They climbed a mound and leapt across a stream, their clothes spattered with earth.

Severo had trouble keeping up with Serena. They arrived at a shady plateau and Severo, out of breath behind her, looked about for the golden glimmer of treasure, the sparkle of diamonds, noting the landmarks by the light of the moon to be sure of finding the same spot tomorrow, but there was nothing shimmering around him.

In the middle of a clearing, a pale light shone on a giant tree, its trunk covered in flowers.

'This is the oldest tree in the area,' said Serena. 'The only real treasure in the forest.'

Severo Bracamonte gazed at the flowers cascading down the trunk, the strong bark, the branches rising up towards the sky. The tree stood before them like a man. The trunk was so wide they could not have got their arms around it.

At the sight of the tree, Severo was disappointed, almost annoyed, but Serena's interest in botany spurred him to lyricism, and he decided to show off a little.

He spoke a few bucolic words which sounded a bit like poetry. Serena was touched by his sensitivity.

Forgetting the tree, Severo made a point of telling her how much he enjoyed having a girl like her around on the farm, and he expressed himself with such gratitude and elegance that she blushed and exclaimed with a note of warmth in her voice, 'Let me know when you next go digging.'

*

From that moment on, the two of them became close. Serena came back to the shed the following day and the days after it, opening the door without knocking, always following the same rituals.

She brought roasted hazelnuts, lemon cakes, plates of sliced fried banana and sweets Candelaria Otero had conjured up in her kitchen.

Severo had little to offer in return, but greeted her with generous enthusiasm. When she arrived he would stand and move about, showing her drawings, summarising books, asking her questions and answering them in the same breath.

He once told her the story of how the pirate François l'Olonnais had pillaged the town of Maracaibo, whose attics were filled with gems, and the buccaneers had feasted for two weeks. He told her he had navigated the Sargasso Sea, floating above a famous ship graveyard where chests of gold lay hidden inside the wrecks. Like a dreamer or a poet, he didn't hesitate to tell her tales as if he had lived them, in order to impress her. He even shamelessly assured her that he could calculate longitude without a chronometer by judging the distance between the edge of the moon and a star.

Certain that a glorious future lay ahead of him, he saw prophetic signs everywhere he looked.

'Look at my left hand,' he would say, lifting his arm. 'You can see how itchy it's been these past few days. Everyone knows that's a good omen.'

Circumstances drew them together. They soon began to head into the forest together, each on the trail of his or her quest. Like two alchemists, one carrying the set square and the other the compass, they crossed fords and scaled slopes. They walked side by side, arm in arm, full of innocent hope, like the first day of creation.

They were sure that sooner or later their efforts would be rewarded by the appearance of an undiscovered plant or a rusty chest. While Severo tried to interpret the beeps from his metal detector, Serena sought to solve the enigmas of the undergrowth.

Should Serena need to come up with a name for a new variety of flower, Severo suggested those of corsairs and filibusters. If Severo found shells on his path, Serena explained it was good luck to find them so far from the beach.

Sometimes they stayed in the woods together until the sun went down, to avoid the afternoon heat. Severo would find a comfortable spot, sit on the ground, unbutton his boots and clean his metal detector.

Serena, in a crumpled dress, sheltering under a satin umbrella, her legs crossed over a stone, chin held high, queen of all she surveyed, listened as he railed against the black marketeers who made false gold by debasing it with copper filings.

'I don't want to fool anyone, Serena. If I keep digging, I'll find Henry Morgan's treasure eventually. I haven't crossed the entire country just to track down a legend.'

Serena smiled. If Severo remained disappointed, their outings were fruitful for her. She never came home empty-handed.

Here was a flower. There, a rare insect. She showed him how she caught butterflies hidden in the nasturtiums, how she made a pulp from the leaves of the calabash tree, and explained her way of interpreting the science of the stars.

Every now and then, she would gaze at the countryside around them and say, 'Just think – the orchids planted in the gardens of kings come from here.'

And Severo would stare at the horizon and reply, 'The gold for cathedral vaults comes from here.'

In this way, they passed from jealous solitude to trusting camaraderie. Over the months that followed, they grew closer.

One day as they were returning home along the far side of the river, Severo tried to take Serena's hand. Without saying a word she shied away, but as their fingers brushed together they were both surprised at the strength of feeling the touch aroused.

They were interrupted by a weak sound coming from the detector, which soon grew louder and more sustained. The needle on the potentiometer suddenly began swinging from side to side.

Severo put on the headset, walked a metre onwards, then two, drunk on hope, and suddenly, following the sound as quickly as he could, found himself standing at the foot of the giant tree they had come to on their first outing together.

A thousand flowers shone on its trunk. The tree looked smaller than it really was, more fragile. Big black clouds were forming in the sky. A cool wind was blowing from the interior.

Severo Bracamonte took out his pickaxe, turned to Serena and declared triumphantly, 'There's a metal object beneath the tree.'

Serena Otero came to a standstill and stared at him with fear in her eyes.

'It would be a crime,' she cried.

Severo protested gently. He circled the trunk, holding the metal detector and concentrating on the sound coming out of his headphones. He made some small effort to calm Serena down.

'We can plant a thousand trees with what we find underneath this one.'

Enraged, she didn't answer him. She took a few steps forward to touch the bark before turning to stand between Severo and the trunk, as if protecting a child.

'If you uproot this tree,' she said, placing a finger over her heart, 'let your pickaxe strike here first.'

Her tone made Severo Bracamonte drop his metal detector. He blew out a long breath by way of reply, kicking his foot against a large rock.

Unsure of how to react, he spoke of his destiny and passion, reminding her that he was a gold-digger and, like anyone else who shared his calling, would only truly become a man when he had extracted treasure from deep inside the ground.

Serena stared long and hard at him, unblinking, and replied with wisdom and pride beyond her years, 'Imbecile. You'll become a man when you extract treasure from deep inside my eyes.'

Far from flattering him, these words stung Severo. He thought Serena was trying to put him off his mission. He fumed silently, but did his best not to let it show.

The storm broke. He didn't touch the tree, but left to take refuge in his shed. That night, it rained so hard Severo felt as if his heart was bleeding out.

VI

When Severo Bracamonte woke up thinking about Serena the next day, he could not get her words out of his head.

He was not used to being spoken to so frankly, but had to admit he liked it. There had been no sensational revelation shouted at the sky, but a discovery made quietly, like leaves fluttering, like springtime blossoming inside him. Overwhelmed by the memory of the moment, he did not try to deny the new feeling gradually taking hold of him.

From then on, his treasure hunt was no longer focused on treasure. His extensive research turned into numerous excuses to stay on the farm. He was leaving the days of silent excavations and solitary nights in the forest behind him.

Their walks together had sharpened unexpectedly powerful appetites in him, and little by little his obsession and passion for scouring the area became no more than a means of winning Serena's heart.

He suddenly found natural beauty in the contours of her face, which had seemed so ordinary until then. He wanted to know her childhood misdemeanours, what sheets she had slept in, what dresses she had worn. He even wished some accident would befall him, in order to attract her attention. He wanted to be ill to make her worry for his health.

But Serena, seeing how Severo had fallen under her spell, took cruel pleasure in remaining mysterious. She made him wait out of ignorance, pride or fear. When Severo brought up the moment they first met, she was vague, cool and distant. One evening, he came to offer her a partridge he had trapped, but she told him caged birds brought bad luck.

Little by little, Serena grew more stubbornly withdrawn, seeming ever more secretive and indifferent. She silently mocked his tales of afternoons by the river, the adventures of gold-diggers, hands touching under the guava trees.

She recoiled from his advances like a plant from too much light. And when Severo, scarlet with embarrassment, finally asked her why she was behaving in this way, hinting at his nascent feelings, she replied with characteristic calm, 'If they are roses, then they will flower.'

It was at this time that Serena Otero left her childhood behind her. She was now at an age when she would listen to the women in the kitchen telling stories about their men in great detail – tales of proud members, heavy breathing, spontaneous encounters in the fields, passions no sooner born than spent. Sometimes, marriages were celebrated barely nine months before the birth of a child.

Illuminated by these confidences, Serena found herself with new-found longings.

As October drew to a close, a feeling took hold of her. She had a burning desire to see Severo. He was the man she knew best and the only one to whom she had said, without struggling to find the words, what she had always kept from her parents. The warm climate, the years of waiting, the respect he showed her: all of these bewitched her somehow and, by thinking of him all day, she found him suddenly more virile in her dreams.

On the eve of 1 November, she came to find him at the mill. The evening sky was red. Severo was working alone at the sugar press, surrounded by large cogwheels, spraying water over the bagasse and throwing the canes into a roller.

He was stirring the molasses in copper vats when he saw Serena come in, her hair loose. She quickly closed the door behind her, slowed her movements and, affecting languor, said, 'It's a long time since we walked together.'

Severo was thrown. In the face of his silence, she added, 'It's a shame!'

She circled the machine. Unnerved, Severo tried to guess the meaning of her gestures, anxious to avoid making a false step. He asked her if she would like to go for a walk that same evening.

'Not tonight,' she exclaimed.

Then she smiled and murmured tenderly, 'We're fine where we are.'

She wasn't wearing silk stockings under her dress, like the first day they met. The smell of the presses hung in the air. Candles were strewn about on shelves. Sugar trickled along the earthen floor, covered in dry grass.

She took his hand and Severo, astonished, did not pull it away. They exchanged no words, but stood facing one another, almost touching, their mouths half open and pupils dilated.

Suddenly Serena stepped back and removed her clothes without looking away, her eyes filled with both desire and fear. When she was completely naked, she hid her modesty with one hand, making the fan of hairs where her legs met resemble a smile.

Light glinted on her skin like pearls on white satin. Her breasts were alabaster, like those of the Diana statue. She ran her hands flirtatiously over her body before the mirror of his eyes, before blushing at her own daring.

Severo quivered nervously. At the sight of his first naked woman he stood open-mouthed, entranced, ignorant of how to react. Though he knew nothing of the mysteries of women, he summoned his courage, determinedly brought his face close to hers and kissed her.

The kiss was coloured with gold and honey. Its scent carried the vanilla notes of pineapple and her lips smouldered with herby freshness and agave flavours, exuding heat as if she had a flame in place of a heart.

In a whirlwind of emotion, Severo was both

transported and filled with doubt. He tried to go gently and move delicately, but at the sound of Serena's heart beating against her chest he could not contain himself.

This virgin skin burnt against his own. The warmth of her neck gave off a smooth nutty scent. All these months of complicity, of joint endeavours and secrets shared under the cover of the trees, had aroused wild desires in him. And now here she was before him, surrendering.

Serena, as if possessed, could not control herself. Her senses were exploding, causing jerks, spasms and groans of pleasure. She bit, scratched, felt faint. She tried not to cry out, pushed Severo away, but despite herself found her arms pulling him back towards her.

The smell of him excited her even more than his caresses. Severo took her awkwardness for boldness and gave her the pleasure she would not give herself. She had never felt such pain between her legs and for a long time forgot it, until the day much later when flames tore through the field of sugar cane by the farm and she felt, but did not understand, the same burning in her belly.

The two of them lay panting on the bare ground. Severo propped himself up on his elbow and looked at Serena more closely than ever before. As he studied her, her blouse undone with one side covering her chest, she was so perfect he wished she were made of marble so that time would never leave its trace on her skin.

He felt he could tell her everything without saying

a word. At that moment, naked in the mill amid the heady scent of old barrels, it seemed to Severo Bracamonte that this woman had invented love itself.

That first time was followed by a long siesta during which he dreamed of Captain Henry Morgan. The same thing happened at the same time every day for twenty years, with British punctuality, and he never tired of conjuring up corsairs and heroic disasters at sea.

He didn't snore. Instead, he made the sad creaking sound of a shipwreck, which sometimes made Serena, lying on the other side of the bed, think of salt and sea spray.

For ten years after they had given each other the painful joy of passage to adulthood, Severo Bracamonte could not imagine any man on earth luckier than he, and perhaps in his bolder moments, he understood that his treasure had always lain in a place out of reach of his imagination.

He felt so at ease with the family that the very next day he repaired the rotten roof of the hut. He made an awning and cut cinnamon wood which, in his opinion, held nails better than walnut. He even thought of making *tablopan*, a wood substitute made with crushed sugar canes, and everyone applauded this environmental initiative.

Señor Otero took him on as an apprentice and taught him the art of the harvest. Though Severo was not strong, his unbending will and amorous enthusiasm spurred him on. Work began at daybreak. He would cut the canes as low as possible, cleaning off the leaves and bundling the canes together. Sometimes grubs tunnelled through the stems and they had to be thrown away at once.

Severo kept his head down, cutting away, his back curved in effort, and could claim to know which canes to fell from smell alone. With great sweeps of the machete he chopped, sliced, piled up, and when the time came to return to the mill, he left the field looking as if a storm had passed through.

These were the days of slash-and-burn farming. The fields were set alight to drive away snakes and dispose of the leaves, giving the first batches of rum a burnt-cane flavour that made them unique in the region.

Otero explained the various cutting systems. He showed Severo how to build a fire, striking a match and setting light to a piece of bark before carefully feeding the flames with dried grass, ensuring the fire was contained.

'Sugar cane is like hope,' Otero would say. 'You have to burn it to allow it to grow back stronger.'

The whole village came out to watch the fires. Looking up at the sky, they could see reddish smoke swirling up from the surrounding farms to mark the end of one harvest and the beginning of another.

The villagers took the opportunity to throw wobbly tables and chairs and broken cartwheels into the fire. Laundry strung up to dry between branches was specked with grit like black pepper, and the molasses were thick with ash.

Severo Bracamonte realised he loved the land more than he loved gold. After heavy rains, the path flooded and became covered in mud. It took a team twice as big to move the carts, which were still pulled by mules. Severo dug channels to drain away the water and allow a passable road to be built.

He took his tools with him wherever he went. When the lamp oil ran out, he would coat the wicks in his own pressed cocoa butter. He oversaw the production of the molasses as zealously as he had pursued his treasure hunt, so that no blade of straw was ever found in the juice extracted from the canes.

He soon learnt how to use the residue left in the vats, the froth that spilt out and the honey-coloured remnants to distil a basic cane alcohol.

He wanted to make rum. He made a still out of a pressure cooker, some buckets and a copper coil. He enjoyed slowly putting the pieces of apparatus together, studying the systems of condensation and backflow.

He took a childish pleasure in watching the alcohol vapours rising to the lip of the still and then passing through the coil submerged in a barrel of cold water, a process by which he obtained a rather poor, rough-tasting, undrinkable spirit that he presented as an oriental drink.

Although the family usually went into the village on

horseback, on Sundays they headed to Mass on foot. The mother hid her hair under a large mantle and Serena covered her shoulders with a lace bolero.

Out of gratitude to the family, Severo went with them to church. Genuinely happy to accompany them, he sat at the back and, while the priest recited the communion prayers, compared the Virgin statues to Serena, convinced that this mystical fusion of plaster and flesh had lain here waiting for him since birth.

These were happy years for Serena Otero too. She hung pots of flowers everywhere about the house, put on music and changed the colour of the curtains to let the light in. She hung cherries over her ears as earrings and let the sun bronze her shoulders.

Far from prying eyes, she arranged to meet Severo in the forest and rolled with him on the yellow earth, scratched by the thorns, laughter mingling with kisses in their mouths. She believed herself to be alone, separated from the world by the strength of her passion, suddenly brought out of herself. She was surprised to find herself repeatedly looking in the large nutmeg-wood mirror in the corridor, and her face would light up with a slight smile and a look of supreme happiness as she recalled her afternoons with Severo.

On the first day of November that year, the little old lady appeared. Holding an empty bucket, she crossed the living room without a word.

Carrying her cinnamon wine and candles in a bag,

she locked herself in the back room to mourn her late husband as usual, emerging again several hours later, the bucket filled with tears. She looked older, more hunched, the lace of her clothes more worn.

On her way out, she made sure to tell Señor Otero, as she had done each year for the past twenty, 'See you next year, Señor.'

But Ezequiel Otero, sitting in his wing chair, would not see her the following year. His last few months had been overshadowed by a fall in the price of molasses, a late harvest and serious health problems.

He died suddenly of a brain haemorrhage at the beginning of the dry season, when the guava trees were sagging under the weight of their fruit. His wife, Candelaria, survived him by only a few days, and the two velvet-draped tin-handled coffins were placed side by side, as silent now as they had been in life.

Out of respect, Serena Otero dressed in black and planted an aloe between the two tombs, according to Caribbean custom.

But she did not remain in mourning for long; a few weeks after the Oteros' passing, Severo Bracamonte proposed a marriage of convenience for the purposes of the inheritance.

It was a small but proper ceremony, with a priest and gardenia crowns. Severo put on a white felt suit with silver embroidery, a pearl-grey tie and wore a pocket watch on a bronze leontine chain. Serena wore a dress with a train, white satin heels and gloves with two buttons at the wrist. She had plaited her hair around a chignon studded with lilies, and a veil dyed in a saffron bath fell over her shoulders.

The guests arrived in the afternoon. The church altar was decorated with the same white roses Serena painted for her herbariums. The Mass was celebrated under the arches of the nave amid the scent of myrrh, and the married couple went out onto the front steps to greet their guests.

They were congratulated outside the church in the village's only square, where a horse-drawn carriage used to transport maize awaited the newly-weds.

They began work on the family home straight away, but they were soon forced to put it up for sale. Their savings were not enough to replace the equipment.

Severo had the idea of taking over the mill and setting up a distillery, and Serena wanted to restore the withering plantations to their former glory. No buyer was ever found, and the house remained in the name of Bracamonte.

VII

So Serena Otero became Serena Bracamonte and, as was customary at the time, took on the running of the household following the death of her parents. The young couple moved into the upstairs bedroom in which mother and father had exchanged notes on loneliness for sixty years.

It was a spacious room with a large window overlooking the garden. There were pastels on the walls with grey crepe around the frames and a dressing table made of lignum vitae. Serena hung pressed flowers on the walls, placed vases of narcissi on top of chests of drawers and planted a papaya tree in a large pot to protect the house from unwanted spirits.

Now that Severo Bracamonte had a family mission to fulfil, he no longer thought about treasure. The desire to find life in his wife's belly soon made him forget the gold in the bowels of the earth. But nature had other ideas, and Severo was abruptly forced to see that even in love, you can't have everything.

They tried every possible fertility ointment and balm. Some claimed the answer lay in drinking manatee blood; others, the husband's urine. A highly respected scholar told them to take a portable stove to the coast and boil up mineral salts.

Severo travelled to the nearest port but only found fishermen who sold him a chrysocolla, a green and blue stone from Chile whose energy, they said, encouraged ovulation.

Serena made sure her food was well cooked and limited her caffeine intake. Her female neighbours made her potions from powdered quince, mountain rose and three ounces of mugwort. They advised her to avoid the gaze of men bitten by snakes, or dreaming of broken mirrors.

They brought in a healer who buried women up to their shoulders under a full moon, with honey between their legs. It was said that the curlew's song foretold a pregnancy, and Serena spent many hours listening out for the call of this bird she had never seen. Despite everything, she fell pregnant only once, without knowing it, but the embryo lived barely an hour inside her womb.

A dull state of repressed anxiety arose between her and Severo like an unspoken pact.

Serena, who had inherited her mother's love of cooking, brought lime-scented rice and bacon-wrapped prunes to the table. At breakfast, there was strong black coffee with a slice of rye bread and a knob of butter. At lunch, one hundred grams of meat, beetroot, whose nutritional qualities she extolled, and three glasses of Madeira.

Before going to bed, Severo Bracamonte had acquired Ezequiel Otero's habit of taking to his rocking chair to smoke a pipe.

It was a time of modernisation for the village. As the river was navigable, a port was built around the first landing stage, which became a docking place for the pirogues carrying sand for building sites. A sign mounted on a dry-earth wall gave the price of wood for the boats' furnaces.

As trade flourished, the land was divided up, with plots going for fifteen cents a square metre. The road was widened to make room for the first tramline. At nightfall, fourteen street lamps forged in Brazil lined the main road – an effort to discourage both the criminal and the carnal.

Families moved close to the river, but water pollution pushed them back from the banks and for several years there were cases of malaria.

Severo was not yet thirty years old, but looked fifty. Everything he had heard, learnt and discovered was engraved upon his memory. He had a perfect understanding of harvest techniques, the mysteries of the sugar press and how to pile up the many barrels that were beginning to be counted and numbered.

He knew how some made their fortune, understood the liquor business, the coopers' craft and traders' corruption, but what really interested him was rum production. He had long since stopped thinking about treasure, to the extent that when a magpie came carrying a gold tooth in its beak, he barely thought of Henry Morgan.

Little by little, the plantation became a distillery. Despite his limited expertise, Severo Bracamonte planted thousands of sugar canes which grew into a forest on hillsides where before there had been nothing but snakes.

The cane was cut by by hand by dozens of mulattos whose badly drafted contracts were signed with a faltering cross and remained in force for a hundred years.

He had heard the story of a marquis who had once brought two camels over from Egypt to transport bundles of sugar cane. They had been found dead, killed by snakebites. The tale had led him to buy Abel and Cain, two bulls whose stamina had led to his herd doubling in size in the space of two years.

The canes were crushed in a mill and the dry bagasse served both to feed the fire beneath the still and to nourish the cattle. A portion of the molasses was left to age in amburana-wood barrels which gave the finished spirit notes of nutmeg and clove, pepper and cinnamon.

And so with a combination of discipline, order and pluck, Severo Bracamonte set an admirable example of national production not seen since the sorry days of the Spanish missions.

'Rum? But that's for slaves and servants,' people mocked.

'Rum,' replied Severo, 'is the gift of this land.'

Severo Bracamonte decided that in order to make a top-quality product, he needed to team up with a liquor company. He learnt to be patient, since he could only start selling what he made two years after harvesting it. The correct strain of yeast had to be selected, the liquid distilled several times, and then it was filtered with charcoal and coconut shells.

The liquor company insisted the alcohol be aged in heavy black Limousin oak barrels stamped with yellow labels with red borders. Severo had to order them from black-market dealers who sold him charred bourbon barrels from the United States, previously used for port and sherry.

Suppliers and estate owners came knocking at the door of the farm where rum was aged in soleras, the barrels piled four high and the oldest alcohol blended in to improve the young.

He greeted them from a large high-backed armchair he'd had shipped over at great cost.

'And yet,' Severo would say, 'the best place to store rum is between one's back and one's chest.'

His business soon expanded considerably. The farm spread up the banks to where the rivers merged. Huts were turned into stables, the weir into a water mill, the house into a three-storey mansion surrounded by a terrace planted with mimosas, where sheep were bred for feast days.

Severo Bracamonte, who now employed around twenty workers and owned a five-hectare plantation, had ideas of setting up a cooperage.

It was around this time he grew a moustache. Ahead of his time, he rubbed it with rosewater lotion and slicked the ends. Casting all modesty aside, he liked to say the words 'Master rum-maker' proudly to himself, without quite knowing what they meant.

He carried on making rum until the end of his life, but never knew how to talk about it. Though he could distinguish almost two hundred colour variations in the molasses, judging whether an alcohol had 'body', 'personality' or 'character' seemed part of a rhetoric reserved for more distinguished men.

He had a knowledge of sugar growing no book could have given him, but was content simply to make nice amber bottles with straw woven around the neck and a red cap over the cork. Like any peasant made good, he was superstitious and 'christened' his rum with two drops of water before resealing the barrel.

His new profession had stopped him scrabbling in the earth. He was no longer the gold-digger of yore. Nowadays the discipline of his work was enough to fulfil him and every afternoon after lunch he would sit in an oak chair, drink a glass of rum and reflect on the morning's achievements. He would allow himself to nod off, surrounded by the scent of camphor and almond blossom. Sometimes in the calm of night he found himself feeling nostalgic for his past. When people reminded him of the adolescent who had dreamed of fabulous treasures and an extraordinary destiny, he hardly recognised himself. It was a long time before he could see his childish illusions as marks of the glorious confidence of youth.

All he had kept from that time was his unconditional love for Serena. In his eyes, she was still the rebellious, passionate girl who made his dreams seem noble, the girl who had stood between him and the tree. She was the only person in the village he would allow to have the last word.

When she swept back her hair, he could still see the stubbornness of youth on her brow. She had not lost her freshness, her camellia complexion or the expressiveness of her body, and he went on loving her without asking to be loved in return.

The couple understood one another without needing to say so. Since those first embraces in the mill, they had left behind two lonely existences to follow one long and winding romantic path, walking side by side or standing face to face, united only by the quirk of fate that had brought Severo to the house and given Serena the strength to keep him there.

They lived a quiet life without happiness or grief and this state of surrender suited them as the reward for past battles.

In bed, Severo never imagined himself in the arms of another woman, and Serena, by nature more distant than her husband, gazed at him with a fierce warmth that might have been love.

Serena Bracamonte was never able to shake off the feeling she was living in the wrong world. Nevertheless, she helped with the rum making, blanching orange-tree leaves and pouring the mixture into gallon buckets to make syrups. She made colourings with caramel and infusions of cloves, tar and scraps of tanned leather.

She also looked after the accounts, the transaction

register and contracts, and ended up acquiring a head for business. But this line of work didn't interest her. She had a natural inclination for the arts and wished to study painting and literature. She became interested in the Grand Masters, comparing skies painted in different periods, and then in Romantic writers and it seemed to her that she lived in an era overflowing with poetry.

So few books reached the village that as soon as they entered the house, Serena felt compelled to read them that same night. These were the days of serialised love stories, with twists and turns to raise the eyebrows of Love itself.

She read not what she wanted but what she found to read. As books often came to her without their covers, she never knew which author had written that heart-rending novel about a young woman with impossible dreams. And since the last pages were missing, she never had to weep over the death of Emma Bovary, or the idea of killing oneself for love.

She read La Fontaine, who always lifted her spirits. One night, she told Severo that if the rum business ever stopped being profitable, they should think of investing in breeding hens.

'For the golden eggs, of course!' she exclaimed.

It took Severo Bracamonte another twenty-five years to understand the joke.

These books taught Serena about servitude and revolt, infidelity and crime, the magic of a description and the pertinence of a metaphor. They gave her a nuanced understanding of masculinity, about which she had known almost nothing. She learnt that the Tower of Pisa leaned, that a wall ran across China, that some languages had died and others were yet to be born.

At the age of twenty-seven, she was graceful and elegant, the delicacy of her gestures contrasting with the coarseness of those around her. She employed a servant girl, though she barely needed her.

One unusually cool evening, she declared she would have liked to live in a country where people wore scarves and looked forward to the arrival of spring. She dreamed of winter as if it were nature's masterpiece. To her, winter was a magnificent scene peopled with women wearing coats, fur hats and fox-fur stoles around their necks.

She swallowed the old cliché that writers could spend hours debating the placement of a comma, and that a single verse might occupy them for years. She longed to spend evenings discussing current affairs while smoking foreign tobacco, and assumed the habits of a class she had not come from, but which she now considered her own.

The radio was left on all day. A bulletin service broadcast updates from around the world. One day at two o'clock in the afternoon came the news that for the first time in history, a TV station was showing an advertisement.

The advert was for Bulova, a brand of watches. 'America runs on Bulova time!' It lasted ten seconds exactly and had cost four dollars to make. The Venezuelan radio presenter broke the story as if announcing a sensational headline, recounting this huge step forward in great detail and concluding, 'Latin America runs on Bulova time too!'

The notion of progress became so firmly lodged in Severo Bracamonte's mind that the very same day he resolved to set up his cooperage. He refused to carry on buying pre-made barrels and crates of supplies from black-market companies.

It was Serena who wrote the advertisement for local radio. She did not use a pseudonym as she had done before, but felt a sweet sense of nostalgia as memories of long-lost illusions returned.

Her advert called for a professional cooper and gave details of the salary and conditions. And this time, despite the fact her appeal was read out only once, she was not kept waiting long. Two days later, she received a response.

VIII

Such was village life when the Andalusian arrived. He had crossed the valley on a black horse accompanied by a local guide, and a train of mules bearing a collection of calfskin-bound books.

When he reached the Bracamonte house, he jumped down from his horse, tied the bridle to a branch and carefully placed an armful of hay under the beast's nose.

He was a Spaniard in his sixties with hair like a mole's pelt, a broken nose and arched eyebrows which, when raised, gave him an aristocratic air. He had the weathered brown hands of one who works the land, with square fingernails and, on his fourth finger, a signet ring inherited from his father and engraved with what he claimed was the family crest.

The memory of some long-held grief made his eyelids droop halfway down his eyes. He might have passed for handsome had time not softened and blurred the features of his face, but he still looked the part in a clean made-to-measure suit which suggested a man of taste. A cut above the average traveller, he wore a cravat and topaz pin around his white collar, a tartan waistcoat in the British style and, in the buttonhole of his jacket, a white metal pig symbolising good fortune.

Severo Bracamonte had not expected to see a cooper so smartly dressed. He invited him into the living room. The Andalusian was holding a yellow dog named Oro on a lead, the beast's low tail trailing behind him and sweeping across the gravel as he walked. Raising his muzzle, he sniffed the flowers around the front steps. Apparently unfazed by the insects dancing around him, he was a loyal servant who rarely strayed from his master, constantly raising his head and fretting if he found himself any distance away from the Andalusian.

When Oro saw Serena he barked once. She jumped, explaining she was not fond of dogs. The Andalusian came to the dog's defence.

'You've nothing to be afraid of. This dog is as quiet as a cat.'

To make conversation, he began listing Oro's merits. The animal had only been brought across the Atlantic on a coaster to hunt pigs on the islands, but upon his arrival, he had smelt a gold coin and it had since been claimed he had a gift for sniffing out treasure. Severo was amazed.

'You should be flattered,' he told Serena, pointing to the animal. 'This dog has been trained only to bark at gold.'

The dog's owner felt the need to clarify. 'But for now, he's yet to bark at treasure.'

Serena took the remark personally, pursing her lips.

'I've still got work to do, then.'

The Andalusian tried to strike a diplomatic note.

'He's just biding his time.'

This seemed natural to Severo, who replied, 'Only dogs of good pedigree know how to wait.'

'Still, I'd like it if he barked a little more often,' the other man sighed with a wry smile.

Serena contemplated the two men bowing and scraping, taking it in turns to compliment one another. She asked the Andalusian, 'And have you found any treasure yet?'

'Not yet.'

She shrugged.

'The dog has been trained to look for gold,' she said. 'If you haven't found any, why should he bark?'

The two men told her she didn't understand and continued to gaze at Oro in admiration. The Andalusian, who thought of the dog as a son endowed with a soul, concluded, 'He doesn't bark, but I sometimes feel he's about to speak.'

The clock struck midday. They sat down for lunch. The Andalusian took off his hat, tidied his things and washed his hands. When he took off his jacket, Severo noticed the elastic garters holding his shirtsleeves up above the elbow and thought this must be some new European invention.

The man spoke about wood, iron, the porosity of oak, 'the angel's share'. He explained how oxygen worked on alcohol. His gestures were polite, delicate and considerate. The conversation warmed up. He soon confessed that his true passion was not making barrels. Severo, listening intently, was curious. The Andalusian said he liked going out on digs and had undertaken a few little expeditions, unsuccessful but exhausting all the same. But this, he said, was the price you had to pay to become a 'self-made man', a phrase he proudly pronounced in English.

'Still, it's ironic to think that a "self-made man" is nothing more than a man kneeling in a muddy river trying to find some meaning in life.'

'A muddy river?' asked Severo, taken aback.

'Of course, that's where you can expect to find big surprises.'

This sparked something in Severo. The stranger had an understated charm about him. He spoke as though feeling his way, approaching the subject in a roundabout fashion.

'And you're travelling wherever the road takes you, Señor?' asked Severo, intrigued.

'On the contrary,' replied the Andalusian. 'The great adventurers are my guides.'

'Marco Polo? Cook? Bougainville?'

The Andalusian smiled. He mentioned the names of Francis Drake, l'Olonnais, the Baron de Pointis and Oexmelin. Severo's eyes kept widening. And when the visitor brought up the legend of Jean Lafitte and his chests of gold in the sands of Louisiana, near Calcasieu Lake, Severo Bracamonte had a kind of revelation.

Then the Andalusian added, 'But why look so far afield? Let's take the example of Henry Morgan.'

Severo had to restrain himself. At last he asked the question Señor Otero had once addressed to him, on the night of his arrival, and which was now burning on his lips.

'So, do you have gold?'

Silently the Andalusian took from his pocket a little leather purse secured with an alligator's tooth and pulled out a yellowish stone wrapped in a handkerchief.

'There are three ounces here,' he said, pointing to it with his finger.

In the middle of the man's palm sat a piece of golden metal barely larger than an olive pit, at which they all stared in silence.

Severo shivered. As far back as he could remember he had only ever known iron, the hard and heavy metal used for ploughshares, wheel rims, barrel hoops and bulls' nose rings. For the first time he had before him soft, fragile gold, shining in the darkness, with tooth marks in it. He had spent so much of his youth searching for the stuff, had striven so hard to find it, that the sight of it now in the lamplight, looking almost worthless, could only disappoint him.

Serena, on the other hand, saw immediately that the Andalusian had never made a single barrel in his life and that his coming here was a coincidence unconnected to the advertisement she had placed. This was the second time a man had come to her table to speak of a treasure she had never seen. She would have liked to take her husband aside to speak privately with him, but since Severo was chewing his lips,

103

apparently deep in thought, it was she who spoke first.

'You haven't come here by chance, Señor,' she said. 'What is it you wish to propose?'

The Andalusian calmly spread a number of maps of islands on the table along with some Indian-ink sketches and cracked compasses. There were arrows and markers, degrees of latitude and illegible inscriptions scribbled all over the papers. The maps had come from the archives of a cathedral in London, collected, he said, by a priest. Then, pointing vaguely at the documents, he said, in a Spanish so old-fashioned it was close to Latin, that the treasure must be somewhere hereabouts, between the old sugar mill, the entrance to the forest and the banks of the river.

'I've studied all the geological maps of the area. I've consulted the land registry and pored over the records of neighbouring plots.'

He pointed out various distances and landmarks.

'The river used to be wider, but the bed dried up. It's a matter of searching the banks. I think —'

Severo cut him off. He had the impression he was listening to his younger self and finished the man's sentence, filled with emotion as before.

'You think ... it's not just a legend?'

'Of course,' the Andalusian went on slowly. 'I didn't come all this way to find a family heirloom or a princess's treasure buried at the bottom of a garden. I know my craft.' Then, having drained his glass, he pronounced grandly, 'If the stars were made of gold, I'd dig up the sky.'

Severo was overwhelmed to find such a display of determination and frankness under his roof. At last, here was a man who thought like him, had taken the same journey, and understood him.

Henry Morgan had definitely left his treasure in the region. This stranger's presence was the proof.

He wanted to know more. The Andalusian had landed in the Gulf of Coquivacoa as a volunteer soldier in a battle that lasted only a few months. He was a clockmaker by profession, born among the olive groves in the Spanish province of Malaga. After the war, he had met an artisan who had told him of the treasures to be found in the former colonies. He had gone straight there and found enough gemstones, amber and mineral veins to convince him to stay.

'It's driving me mad,' he confessed.

By the time Severo met him, the travels across great plateaux and stories of good fortune had seeped into the very fibre of his being. He was an energetic man, as wily as a salesman.

He had lived on Cocos Island off Costa Rica, questioning sailors on the treasure of Benito Bonito. He had followed the legend of the hidden treasure of the church of Lima, inspired by the tale of the German August Gissler, who had spent twenty years on the island and died with thirty-three gold coins in his pocket. He also claimed to know the man who had found William Kidd's treasure on an island not far from New York.

'With just half the treasure, I saw this peasant living like a prince.'

The Andalusian had spent many years and several fortunes searching for Blackbeard's gold on the island of Smuttynose off the coast of New Hampshire, to no avail.

He had excavated the depths of Diego Suarez Bay, explored every cavern and interviewed former pirates. He claimed to have once held in his hands the cryptogram belonging to Olivier Levasseur, the pirates' pirate known as The Buzzard. It showed his hiding places on Réunion.

All these journeys had confirmed his vocation. He could no longer think of anything but treasure chests with padlocks hanging off them, secret combinations and spell books covered in cabbalistic symbols, and longed to devote his years of experience to solving riddles.

Severo felt compelled to speak. He talked of his days of assiduous research and told anecdotes that made everyone laugh. They opened another bottle. Wanting to show his visitor the statue of Diana, he led him out to the porch.

'I don't even know how much she weighs,' he said. 'But I do know that if she were even a gram heavier, I wouldn't have been able to carry her back here.'

The Andalusian contemplated the statue with amusement, and said it had most likely been commissioned during the late classical period to adorn a local monarch's corridor. Then, letting his thoughts run on, he imagined a more prosaic destiny for the piece. Diana had probably decorated a courtesan's garden, been left to languish in an obscure museum and finally found herself standing in the rain on the terrace of a naval college. Snatched by pirates during a raid, she might have crossed the ocean among sacks of flour in a frigate's hold and been abandoned inland following a shipwreck. He even tried to date these events, which Severo took as a kind of affront to his only discovery in decades of looking.

In order to regain the upper hand, Severo took out the map he had used to explore the region. Without unfolding it, he waved it in front of his guest and assured him of the accuracy of the markers drawn on it.

He proposed a deal: the Andalusian would fund the expedition while Severo would provide the documents for a share of the booty.

'One often meets dreamers who've spent years studying a map bought for a fortune from some crook,' said the Andalusian. He locked eyes with Severo and added, 'But if I find the treasure thanks to your map, well ...' He gave a wry smile and held out his hand to make a gentleman's agreement. 'Fifty–fifty?'

Severo agreed on condition that the plantations, which were soon to be harvested, be left untouched.

His map indicated that the treasure must have been buried four hundred feet south-west of the forest and thirty feet from the river. In the middle of the map there were symbols representing rocks, with capital letters and arrows pointing in both directions drawn over them.

Without wasting any time, the Andalusian, usually

so elegantly dressed, hastily pulled on an old pair of wellington boots and threw a Mexican shawl over his shoulders, and together they headed into the forest, torches in hand.

The visitor strode triumphantly through the valley with the map under his arm and a compass in his fist. He had with him a single dose of quinine and a dagger in a silver scabbard to protect them from danger.

He gradually realised that the map was not completely accurate. If you went from the north of the forest, the lines met on the riverbanks. If you approached from the south, they intersected a hundred feet further on.

Severo and the Andalusian pored over their papers. They took a few tools out of their bags and began digging with their pickaxes in the late afternoon.

The two men slogged away into the evening, but they were filled with doubts. They returned to the edge of the forest to retrace their steps, making a different calculation of the distances. The Andalusian spread the map in front of him to compare it to the landscape before him.

Severo explained, 'The map is fifty years out of date. Deforestation has changed the landscape and compasses may have been less precise back then.'

The Andalusian could not find his place on the map. There was no stone or rock – it had all disappeared under a damp layer of moss. He was beginning to think the map was a clumsy copy. Severo said nothing, leaving room for doubt.

He knew his forest. He had roamed it like a mad

dog, checking every leaf, every hill, every riverbank. He had probed every hollow tree and sketched out the terrain. He had not been born on this land, but had spent so many years turning it over that he considered it his own. And in all this time, he had found nothing but a woman made of marble.

But while Severo had been breaking his back digging, the Andalusian had perfected his own search methods. He knew how to measure the angle of a star and draw a meridian. His surveys were far deeper and more efficient than holes dug with shovels. He had cut the ends off wooden drill bits and extended them by soldering on steel rods. This meant he could reach a depth of five metres and, if he encountered an obstacle as he went, he would finish the job with a spade.

One day on the riverbank, the metal detector made a faint noise and the rod jarred. Excited, Severo grabbed the pickaxe and started digging furiously.

'Be careful!' the Andalusian shouted. 'You might damage the treasure chest!'

But no treasure was unearthed that day. The hole filled up with water that had to be bailed out. They made a dam to divert the stream, but the ground was sandy and the mud ran between the stones. They tried to cover the opening with sheets of metal but the wind brought them down.

For a fortnight they drained and dug, stopping only to mop their brows and take a swig of rum. They finally excavated a forty-foot tunnel at the bottom of a hill, only to discover that all the detector had picked up was an old ship's cable that had been rusting away for three centuries under the ground.

IX

On 1 November the little old lady came, holding her empty bucket, cinnamon wine and candles. The Andalusian was in the living room studying his maps on a small folding table propped over his lap.

Oro the dog stood up and barked once. The little old lady did not react, but continued on her way without looking up. Slowly but confidently she walked to the room at the back of the house, took the key out of her pocket and entered the room without a backward glance.

These were aimless weeks for the Andalusian, in which he felt lost, achieving nothing, impatient for clues, often raging against the inaccuracy of his maps. He went out panning, but no gold appeared – not a single speck of glitter was left in the bottom of the sieve.

He complained about everything, found the heat stifling, the pork bitter, the villagers sullen. He dug belligerently as if in haste to reach the centre of the earth, leaning on his spade and wiping the back of his sleeve across his brow.

One day when he had taken his shirt off and the sun was shining on his back, Severo noticed a number of scars that looked as if they had been made with a cobbler's awl.

At around seven in the evening, Severo usually invited the other man to join him on the porch for an aperitif. They sat side by side looking out at the countryside as the scent of guavas blew in on the breeze.

'Look at us living the high life,' the Andalusian joked when Severo poured him a second glass. 'Not every gold-digger lives as well as this.'

He reminisced about the hours he had spent up to his knees in mud, sleeping under shelters made of branches and palm leaves on mattresses rolled out on the ground, far from medical supplies, at the mercy of fevers and delirium.

He had always avoided mining regions. He had even turned down plots in Guyana. He said this in a low voice, his hands still, his eyes focused on a point somewhere in the distance, his nostrils quivering, absorbed in his memories.

'At least there's gold to be found there. Here, the land is barren.'

Severo Bracamonte could hardly contradict him. He harked back to his own past, telling his guest how he had turned over every inch of this land. Barren it might be, but he could see now that he had loved gold only to forget it in favour of the long, patient, quiet and humble work of the labourer and master rum-maker.

The Andalusian nodded his approval. Severo went

on to describe how important sugar cane had become to him, how it had made him wiser, teaching him the slow rhythms of nature, and how the plantations had become more precious to him than all the gold in the world. He seemed almost elated.

'No, the land here's not as barren as all that.'

From then on, Severo spent less time in the forest with the Andalusian. The dry season had set in, the slash-and-burn process was beginning and he had to get back to his plantations. As for the Andalusian, he stopped coming to the house so often. Sometimes when he was drawing water from the well, he would acknowledge Serena with a slight nod and she would wave vaguely back at him.

Now thirty years old, she divided her time between her roles as farmer, bookkeeper, wife and housekeeper. Few other women in the region played such a key part in their family's activities.

She had chosen modernity, and fought courageously against the outdated views of her peers. Her voice counted among the village elders and she was called upon to resolve neighbourly disputes. She was known for her charitable work and gave advice to midwives.

Over time, her knowledge became the stuff of legend. She could speak intelligently on subjects ranging from medicine to music to taxes. She studied the life of bees, despite knowing she would never take up beekeeping. She became interested in strange phenomena, seeing in science the miracles of the future. She knew how to return a hard-boiled egg to its liquid state, and was familiar with the mystery of the lobster which changes colour according to its mood.

She was of the opinion that an educated woman could not be forced into submission, and strove less to prove her brilliance than to affirm her freedom.

Outwardly Serena Bracamonte appeared entirely content and fulfilled, but buried in her heart like a ruby in rock were many thwarted joys and stifled passions. She had still not given birth to the treasure she so desired.

When she saw children playing in the street or chasing after one another in the fields, she felt a pang of pain, and her constant grief was written upon her face. She wished she could do the things every mother does: hold her little one tight against her chest, help him take his first steps, play with his hair and whisper tender words in his ear.

This absence of a child only strengthened her desire to be a mother. For years she had contained her fury at being denied motherhood. She was pregnant with emptiness, and cursed the womb that bled with every moon.

Yet for all three of them, a treasure was about to be discovered by unexpected means. It was December. The land lay fallow.

Severo sent out orders to prepare the land for burning in order to start cutting the next day. Torches were lit all around the plantation.

The canes caught very quickly. All at once the fire rose, powerful and upright as a flare, the flames reaching so high the fields could no longer be seen. The heat flattened ferns and twisted tree trunks, and leaves were scorched by acrid smoke.

The fire filled the air with the scent of caramel. It roared like a hundred forges, branches crashed to the ground and the animals in their pens bellowed and let out pitiful cries.

Suddenly a group of horses grazing in the distance were startled by a dark mass passing beneath their hooves. It was Oro the dog, barking and running breathlessly towards the flames. The Andalusian called angrily after him, but though he was shouting at the top of his lungs, the dog disappeared into the inferno.

Then all at once he reappeared, smoking all over, his fur singed. Between his teeth he was holding a half-burnt shoebox.

They all crowded round to look inside. An animal the size of a squirrel, bright red with tawny fur, was curled up asleep inside. It held its shaggy paws either side of its head but the tail was out of sight, presumably tucked under its belly.

It was an innocent-looking creature, its little muscles quivering, its fur singed, covered in ash and bits of branches. It moved slightly, straightened its back and opened its mouth to let out a wild cry. But the noise that came out, somewhere between braying and wheezing, did not come from an animal's throat.

The little body turned over and the face of a newborn baby appeared.

Severo swore loudly. Here was a little girl only a few days old and so dirty she appeared to be covered in fur. Scared by all the faces leaning over her, the child started to wail again so loudly and heart-rendingly that Serena heard it from the house.

When she arrived amid the chaos in the field, Serena saw the little burnt creature in Severo's arms, wrapped in hessian cloth.

She was overwhelmed, filled with emotion, as she had been that first time with Severo in the sugar mill. She took the baby in the crook of her arm, looked at her intently, and an explosion of joy erupted in her belly as if a new life had risen from the blaze to replace her old existence.

Destiny had chosen to save the child from the pyre, but the fire had burnt the left side of her face. A doctor was called from the village and he immediately applied egg white, white flour and aloe vera compresses to her skin to soothe the pain.

A debate arose over the girl's future. Some came down in favour of looking for her parents; others of passing her over to the care of the church. Someone mentioned a boarding school that took in bastard children until they came of age, but Serena Bracamonte objected.

'We're not living in the Middle Ages,' she cried.

She was modern enough in her views to believe that very young children ought to belong to those who found them. She painted a terrible picture of life in an orphanage and made everyone see that to send the little girl there would be unchristian.

'You can stop searching now,' she told Severo and the Andalusian as they gazed at the child in astonishment. 'Here's your treasure.'

The child was laid down to sleep in a wooden crib. No one came forward to claim parentage of the foundling; it was as if the fire itself had given birth to her.

From that moment on, for the second time in his life, Severo forgot about Henry Morgan's treasure. A new being had just entered his life so forcefully that it had pushed out all dreams of finding fortunes.

The next day, the Andalusian decided to leave. He could see there was no longer a place for him in the house. He gathered his belongings, got back on his horse and whistled to Oro, but the dog would not leave the side of the crib where the child was crying under her compresses, wriggling like a worm.

Eventually, to everyone's surprise, he shrugged. 'Let him stay then.' Then he leant down and held out his hand to Severo. 'We will never meet again.'

Two days later a priest came to bless the child. He reminded Serena that orphans should be named according to the calendar of saints, but she refused.

She noted down the date the child had been discovered, as if that were her birthday. She gave her the Bracamonte name, making her part of a dynasty of people carried in on the wind.

And so the child they had found unsought was born a second time under the sign of Cancer, amid the warmth of the mango trees, and they named her after the first woman and the first element: Eva Fuego.

X

The arrival of little Eva Fuego Bracamonte was seen as a bad omen by the local bourgeoisie. As the atmosphere became ever more heated, a rumour went round that the child was Captain Henry Morgan's secret daughter. From then on, the name of the child who had been saved from a burning field, charcoal-black, poor and naked, would forever be associated with piracy.

Serena, on the other hand, had convinced herself that the child was a gift from the heavens. Surely only God could have rewarded her with happiness as profound as the sadness she had felt before.

She loved Eva Fuego more than anybody, as if she were grafted to her. She showered the child with care and attention to make herself worthy of the role nature had denied her. She thanked God for bringing them together, healing the distress of a woman who could not be a mother and the distress of an orphan who could not be a daughter.

For twenty years, Serena held aloe-vera compresses to Eva's temple to relieve the burns. Sometimes when the dressings touched her skin, Eva moaned in pain and Serena was immediately transported back to the blazing fields of sugar cane and the smell of burnt molasses.

Serena's gratitude for the time she spent with Eva was clear to see. She was the last of a line that should have died with her, and with a mixture of admiration and tenderness, devotion and kindness, she gave Eva Fuego the share of love she had never been able to give Severo.

Eva Fuego Bracamonte was baptised by full immersion in Serena's arms, according to the great Babylonian ritual, and from then on they often bathed together. For the first few months of her life, when placed on the bosom of a wet nurse, Eva would bite the breast instead of suckling it, cried a lot, destroyed much of the linen in the house, and her big wide eyes glowered about her.

As an only child, she grew to have an intimate relationship with solitude. Until she was nine, she avoided other children, played with a black rag doll and painted sunflowers with gouache paints on the wood from old barrels. She was both troubled and excited by the world. She was growing up amid the richness and serenity of the landscape, convinced that caterpillars had the gift of speech and believing the trees flew around the birds.

Looking around with still innocent, unfocused eyes, she smelt the soil, breathing in fresh scents never before encountered. She was inspired by everything. The sugar mill was like a giant's kitchen and she often sat licking the scalding bagasse in a corner of the workshop, staring at the red flower blooming in the furnaces and the golden streams running into vats.

Her breath was still that of a small animal, a coati or an armadillo, thick with the hot, harsh scent of humus. She nibbled on flowers, soaking up the innocence of all the creatures around her. Oro the dog never left her side and they played together for hours at a time. Everything was new to her: violent downpours, scarred land, wild waters and the purity of danger. The uncultivated fields were her playground. She ran through the wild grass with tangled hair and grazed knees as if at a party, so that Serena sometimes said, placing her hand on her belly, 'She's so like me.'

Severo Bracamonte was glad to be raising a child in a simple life, far from the vice-filled cities. In the mornings he would take Eva Fuego by the hand and they would go wandering through the quiet, majestic woods, silently taking in views of far-off lands together.

Pressing her cheek against his, she was full of curiosity about her surroundings, trying to catch butterflies and pin them inside a glass box and naming the trees, and to her the world represented a map to be explored, every footstep taking her into virgin territory. Severo spoke to her as the leaves fluttered in the breeze.

He instilled a love of work in her from an early age. He taught her the art of ageing rum, how to oversee the distillation and mark the casks with a stencil. At the age of ten, she learnt to write a barrel's birth certificate, with its year of production and the volume it contained. By twelve, she could already measure out blends and list all the stages in the fermentation process.

Her face grew fuller in time but the burn did not disappear. Serena concocted thick potions of snake flesh and seahorse powder. But Eva Fuego would always carry this mark on the left of her face, from her temple to her jaw, and all her life she was careful only ever to show the world her right profile.

The scar was not all that big, but for a long time she was sure everyone was staring at her, to the extent that she wore scarves wrapped around her head and got used to telling everyone that she had no memory of the accident.

By the time she began putting rags between her legs, Eva Fuego was already solid and quite strong, with a thick black plait that ran all the way down her back. Her knotted brow and her hair seemed to have retained something of the fire that had brought her into the world. She was a sombre character, her mood often charcoal-black, as if the embers of the fire were still smouldering in her soul, and often she frightened herself with the strange force that lay within her.

She dressed in an African style, with silver bangles around her ankles, bracelets around her wrists and swooping necklines to make the farmers blush. She wore flouncy skirts in bright colours, cut as short as she could get away with, made by a local seamstress.

She had a wild, passionate, unpredictable charm

and brazen way about her, and the young men of the village jostled beneath her windows in the hope of catching a glimpse of her through the shutters.

But she was not a girl who appreciated serenades and balconies, mandolins and gallantry. She was a free spirit, more of a Lilith than an Eve. She gained curves and soon became a stout, powerful *morena* with cold features and a despotic stare, with an ability both to raise her voice and impose silence. When she didn't get what she wanted, her fits of anger were implacable.

She looked at men without desire or curiosity, but fearlessly, as if forever trying to square up to them. At the age of fifteen, she looked twenty. By twenty, she was ageless.

Nonetheless, Serena continued to treat her like a little girl. She fussed over her constantly and spoke to her in baby talk. She made compresses for her burns and granted her every whim. To ward off nightmares, she made her eat papaya with the pips in and suck on geranium petals.

She worried about her daughter, calling her fifty times a day and smothering her with attention, and still tried to share the girl's bath, whether Eva liked it or not.

One evening, Serena stripped off beside the steaming bath, adding a little rum to disinfect the water. For a moment Eva Fuego remained still behind her mother without taking off her dress, and watched Serena's planter's hands cutting through the foam.

She studied her thin body, slender waist, small breasts, neat buttocks and fragile thighs. She had never looked at Serena so closely before, and suddenly realised that her mother's body, with its tight muscles and scrawny frame, was nothing like her own.

Never had she been so certain that the blood of another woman ran through her veins. Everything that was different about them suddenly became clear to her: the tone of voice, the way they stood, the way they moved their hands.

She absorbed all this without pain or doubt, but with the tenderness of a girl becoming a woman and seeing for the first time the shadow of a secret surrounding her birth.

From that moment on, she met her mother's kindness with unfettered harshness, to the point that she barely took after her in any way. Perhaps the only habit they shared was that of making the sign of the cross on a child's forehead, or blessing the bread before cutting it.

She turned instead to the women of the village, believing even chit-chat with the washerwomen to be more instructive than a mealtime conversation with her parents. She spent her time with workmen's wives, with gleaners and seamstresses, female market gardeners and women who took in ironing, especially those who had had several children by several deceased husbands.

Eva Fuego saw their breasts, withered from use, their protruding shoulder blades and wizened skin.

She spent hours listening to tales of misspent youth and clandestine abortions. But in all her days, she never found out which of these women had left a shoebox in a blazing field of sugar cane one night after nine months of silence.

Sitting in a circle underneath a tree, those women who couldn't read taught her to interpret oil poured onto the surface of a bowl of water and the wet marks on pebbles, to tell the future in the tea leaves left at the bottom of a cup. In this way they predicted marriages, births and far-off events.

This was how one day, seeing the shape of a gull in a porcelain bowl, Eva Fuego knew she would become a rich woman.

Despite being surrounded by servants, she beat laundry with the local women, crouching on the riverbanks or in the gloom of the wash houses. She accompanied the men piling bundles of canes onto bullocks' backs and sang with them in the evenings after the harvest. When rumours circulated of runaway slaves burning plantations and their masters with them, Eva Fuego applauded the uprising.

By the age of seventeen, she had become what she would remain all her life: a woman whose existence would find meaning only in the pursuit of a pipe dream. She would mount horses, tame spaniels and cut stacks of wood with an axe. The peace and quiet of the forest did little to calm her; on the contrary, it taught her that anything could be made to submit.

One evening, she impressed everyone by managing

to run her hand along the backbone of a wild mare. Her breath, it was said, smelt like gunpowder.

Her very desire to dominate made her indomitable. The only company she kept was Oro the dog, who seemed to her to be as loyal and honest as a brother. But he was old and sick. He weakened with every day he had left to him. He was so skinny you could count his ribs like the rings of an old tree trunk. His hearing had become less sensitive, his eyesight less sharp and his tail less jovial. His tan-coloured fur had gone grey, he had stopped looking up at the slightest sound, and he had even given up licking his lips when given a strip of bacon fat.

Serena kept telling her not to give him so much food. Eva Fuego could no longer stand being constantly watched, and was increasingly irritated by Severo, who always sided with her mother. The bond that had tied the three of them together in the early years seemed to her to have unravelled. They were not cut from the same cloth, and she could see in them no evidence of her own secret, obsessive ambition and feverish drive. When she touched the burn on her face, she felt the wound without knowing its source.

One day Serena walked into Eva Fuego's room and found her sewing a button onto one of her belts. She instinctively hurried across the room to take over the task: Eva Fuego pushed her away. Calm to begin with, but becoming increasingly aggressive, she reproached her mother for her excessive attentions. Serena replied that there was no such thing as excess when it came to love and, raising her voice, told her she was hurt by her ingratitude.

'I'm your mother after all,' she said authoritatively.

Eva Fuego stared back at her.

'You're nobody's mother,' she replied.

Serena was outraged. They argued like never before. Serena was cold and sharp, showering Eva Fuego with petty words like pinpricks.

Eva Fuego remained slouched in her chair. Her skin went bright red, her thick hair swung about, her eyes fizzed with rage like a furious gypsy woman, and her swollen lips spat vulgar words she had learnt on the streets. Serena accused her of associating too much with common people.

'But I'm one of them,' she shouted.

Severo stepped in. He stood between the two women and, using his loudest voice, forced them to be quiet. He tried to make them reach some kind of compromise to restore order to his house. Oro the dog was barking loudly amid all the commotion. When Serena stamped her foot, Eva Fuego leapt up.

'What do I have to do to get some peace and quiet in this house?' she yelled. Then, her face reddened by her scar, she added, 'Burn it down?'

Serena let out a cry and brought her hand to her mouth.

Severo lost his temper. This kind of talk would not do. From now on there would be no more arguments under his roof, and no belt buttons either. He swore this by the statue of Diana who, he said, was the only woman in the house to behave with dignity in these sorry times.

That night, Eva Fuego didn't sleep in her room. She fled to the warmth of the shacks and the welcoming bosoms of the village cooks. She saw at once that she owed nothing to that family, and everything to fate. Sitting in the lamplight amid the overwhelming scent of the almond trees, she had the audacity to believe that it was not her parents who had saved her from the flames, but she herself who had discovered them languishing on a godforsaken farm.

XI

Thirty years earlier, Severo Bracamonte had arrived, a slender, radiant picture of joyful, carefree youth with absolute confidence in the future.

Yet over time he had become as closed as a cask of rum. All that was left of his old laugh was a sad wrinkle that ran across his cheek. His black temples were now sprinkled with dirty snow and exposure to the harsh sun and the rigours of ploughing fields had made his skin as rough as a lizard's.

He expressed what he had become through the movements of his body. His youthful energy had been replaced by the cautiousness of adulthood. He had a softer voice, uglier hands, and the calm strength of a body aware of its own limits.

Yet out of a desire to prove to himself that he was still young, he took on a series of big projects, starting with the approach to the house. He dug and sieved the earth himself. He had the gate on the forest side replaced and a veranda built in wood-imitation concrete. Two lagoons used for fish farming stood between the house and the sandy plains. A row of rosebushes was planted, and a cicada sang in every flower.

Four gardeners worked through the daylight hours. The guava trees lining the driveway were cut into pike, ball and triangle shapes. Stonemasons installed three ashlar steps leading down to a path bordered by fig trees, and Severo insisted on rolling out a carpet of white gravel. He added shutters to make the windows look larger and put up a balustraded pergola, in the middle of which the Diana statue was positioned like a great trophy, all clean and shiny in her mythic pose.

Nobody noticed that the statue was leaning to one side, and in danger of collapsing. There she stood, right outside the house, unsteady and yet unnoticed due to the excitement caused by the completion of the works, which were celebrated with twenty bottles of champagne and a barrel of rum.

Severo was so pleased with the results that he decided to put out a radio advertisement seeking a photographer. Serena immediately set to work on the wording and sent it off, while Severo, beaming with pride, looked forward to framing the picture and hanging it outside.

It was around this time that Oro the dog departed this world. He was declared dead at two in the morning and his body was placed inside a wooden box a metre long and twenty-five centimetres wide built by a certain Carlos Antillano, a carpenter from the island of Margarita.

As he was carried in a modest procession, everyone shared their memories of his Andalusian owner. Eva Fuego was so upset she didn't leave her room for a week.

It didn't take long for Severo to forget old Oro. The improvements to the front of his house made him so happy that he often came to walk around outside, weeding the plant pots and watering the flowers.

One evening as he was strolling around the grounds, he noticed that the Diana statue was standing askew. Since it was late and the workmen were asleep, he tried to right it himself.

He took her by the elbows, forced her right and then left, pushing with his knee, then, suddenly off balance, the statue toppled towards him and fell heavily on his head.

He let out a terrible scream. The lights went on in the porch and everyone came hurrying out.

Severo had been injured on the forehead by Diana's bow and a long stream of blood ran from his scalp straight down to his chin. His head had been sliced open like an apple and was bleeding copiously.

The wound had to be stitched that same night. Barely conscious, Severo tried to fight them off. He had to be physically restrained, strapped down and given drugs and shots of mescal. His hands were burning up, his face was red and his eyes stared upwards.

He slept for three days. Serena was at his side throughout, leaning over the bed attentively. From time to time he coughed, his throat rattled and he complained about everything. His condition was worsening by the hour. Frowning, he refused to eat. Sometimes in the middle of the night he would suddenly stand up, bare-chested, his face deathly

137

pale, and violent spasms would cause his muscles to contract.

Serena would take him by the shoulders and force him to lie back down. As she fanned him and tried to calm him down, he would suddenly fall backwards and lie still, his mouth clamped shut, a continuous grating, whistling noise like an unoiled sugar press coming from his throat. His body was racked with coughing fits and the wound on his head started bleeding again.

He had to be operated on a second time. It was an act of butchery. Serena was so horrified she had nightmares for several days. She felt powerless.

Apothecaries, pharmacists and witch doctors were called in. Several doctors came to Severo's bedside, asked lots of questions, examined him, listened to his heartbeat, wrote out prescriptions and left again, all saying the same thing.

'The best treatment for him,' they said, 'is to keep taking painkillers with a glass of rum.'

When they had gone, Serena would force him to drink her potions. Severo brought up everything he swallowed. He grew weaker and weaker. The room smelt of vomit.

He was given roots macerated in alcohol, soft coral and pearls from Margarita. He had bouts of fever, whined weakly, and his body was drenched in sweat. He gazed at his wife with wordless fear and desperation in his eyes as she humbly asked God to grant her patience and courage.

She and Eva Fuego took it in turns to watch over

him. They changed his bed sheets when he spat out blood. They removed basins, opened the windows and helped Severo to the toilet. The hours passed slowly in this dark, sickly-smelling room. One night, Severo coughed up a large chunk of flesh mixed with lumps of dried blood and Eva Fuego thought he was throwing up his own heart.

In order to speed his recovery, he was prescribed garlic soups with chunks of yam and spoonfuls of holy thistle. Serena was alarmed to see green blotches appearing on his chest, as if life, not wishing to desert him, had instead condemned him to moulder.

He barely spoke, his cough choking him like dust from a beaten carpet. His wild eyes stared into the void and the scar on his brow swelled, cold, dry and black. He had lost so much weight that when he was lifted up, the bones of his pelvis jutted out. When he put his arms around Serena's neck, without saying a word, his eyes seemed to implore her to let him fall into a hole in the middle of the earth.

After a month of struggles and anguish, he was finally able to feed himself again. He began to put a little weight on, but he remained weak. He carried on shivering.

Out of some sense of shame, Severo remained tight-lipped about the causes of the accident. Nobody ever knew how the old man had managed to tip over a marble woman who had never moved in three solitary centuries.

He declared in a state of great distress, 'It's on the

smallest reefs that the largest galleons founder.'

But the accident showed he had reached the age when life becomes a foreign country. His mind was as blunted by the incident as his body. He never really recovered, and this all too brief moment of calm proved to be only a short reprieve before he relapsed.

Eva Fuego walked with him in the garden, pushing his wheelchair, telling him the names of the trees and trying to catch butterflies for him. She often told him stories of pirates and corsairs and treasure hunts to make his heart flutter as it once had.

He would respond with the mixture of enthusiasm and distraction that signals the onset of senile dementia. His memory played tricks on him. When he spoke about rum, everything became muddled in his head – the digs and the statue, the Andalusian and Eva Fuego – like images on the surface of water. He thought Señor Otero was still alive. He walked up and down his veranda, speaking to the statue, whilst yellow iguanas sought patches of sun amid the heady scent of gardenias.

He refused the medicines he was prescribed and tried to carry on working as he had before, but he no longer had the same energy. He tired quickly, like an elderly horse. His raggedy jacket was peppered with dandruff, his cheeks became hollow and his eyes looked bruised. Strands of orangey-grey hair hung down under a rabbit-skin hat.

He seemed to have given up on the idea of living. Sometimes he knelt in the mud, searched the ground with the tip of his machete and filled his pockets with pebbles and worms. He imagined he was finding gold.

The more Serena tried to make him see reason, the more incoherent he became. She showed him the production accounts and papers she couldn't deal with on her own, and he would rave about submitting them to trial by fire to make the invisible ink appear.

This man who had run a group of sugar refineries, who owned numerous hectares of land and had a hundred men working under him, now hung around the old sugar press with a grazing donkey standing by, dressed in rags and tatters, with a thick scar running across his brow, waving his stick in the air. His brain was now no more than an empty chest filled with dust and oblivion, and he had lost the key.

He took to telling everyone he was going to die, and would no longer leave his bed. He asked for paper and ink and began writing letters addressed to no one, encrypting the content, changing his signature and using odd calculations to count up his past expeditions. Then alone at night, by the light of a candle, he would pore over his stacks of documents like a monk at his prie-dieu, still trying to find the treasure he said he could smell in his own bedroom.

On the last day of his life, Severo Bracamonte, who was not a religious man, confessed five times in a row. He insisted on being taken out into the fields to say his goodbyes to the sugar canes, the old mill and the distillery, and see his workers one last time. He promised to keep watch over their endeavours from the hereafter.

Back in his room, he was gagging and struggling for breath. The women rolled up pillows to place under his neck, unbuttoned his shirt and saw marks on his body that resembled a leopard's spots.

They offered him tablets, but he refused them. He wanted one last glass of rum. He pointed to a shelf where an amber-coloured bottle with a gold-rimmed black label stood. When the glass was brought to his trembling hand, he made an immense effort to force himself up on one elbow to drink it, but he felt his heart give way and with his last breath, as the rum spilt over his sheet, said, 'Shit.'

Severo Bracamonte died on a Sunday at the same time as the hens were laying their eggs in the henhouse. None of his loved ones made any comment on his last word, as if the life of hard toil he had led made it fitting for him to utter such a fine obscenity in his final moment of grace.

They kept vigil beside the body for several days and were surprised to find in his will a request for three paupers to be dressed and fed for twelve days, for the salvation of his soul.

A number of men dressed in white came to clean the body and wrap it in a shroud after rubbing it with creams and ointments. Afterwards Severo's mortal remains were purified with lustral water, his face was covered in starch and his jaw tightly bound shut.

His body still fresh, Severo smelt of cut grass. The whole room had the aroma of a lawn, and when he was laid back down on the bed with his head turned north, he seemed heavier. A great inert mass now occupied the room which a light-hearted, devoted and generous man had inhabited for so many years.

As a mark of grief for her husband, Serena covered every mirror in the house with a sheet. She received condolences from the villagers and planted an aloe, as she had done after the death of her parents.

She ordered the mules to be saddled up to take the wreaths to the cemetery and called in Carlos Antillano, the old carpenter who had once measured up for Oro the dog's coffin. He shook her hand kindly and whispered in a broken voice, 'No coffin could contain a man of your husband's stature, Señora Bracamonte. You would do better to have him cremated.'

As a distinguished woman with progressive ideas, Serena agreed that a cremation would be a way of breaking new ground in the village, without disrespecting the dead.

It was 1 November. Golden sun poured down. It was an afternoon so warm that mangoes fell every hour, like cherries in an orchard.

Yet the little old lady did not come that day. Serena wondered if she too had died and the room at the back would remain locked up for ever. The thought did not make her sad. She simply noted it with the same cool detachment with which she would have noticed a book missing from a shelf.

Some metres away from the house, a broad rectangle of pale, untreated wood was placed in the middle of a field of sugar cane and covered in a shroud. The body was covered with a spray of gardenias and a sprinkling of rose petals. Severo's face was as yellow as corn.

A small crowd gathered around the pyre for the duration of the ceremony. Speeches were made and a eulogy was given praising Severo's goodness, dedication and generosity. A man in black lit the torch while reciting the customary holy words, and the flames sent sparks up into the sky.

Eva Fuego did not stay until the end. She kept her distance, knowing already that she would come back here every 1 November to lay a flower in his memory.

Serena was the last to leave. She cried a single tear, as fat and heavy as a drop of molasses. She had already spent a night apart from the man who had slept every night by her side. She told herself that at dawn the next day, thousands of ants would come to take away her husband's remains, carrying them off one by one in a long procession as if tearing apart a sheet of cloth, and on the first evening of her widowhood, she threw onto the ashes the only handful of earth beneath which Severo Bracamonte's soul would rest.

XII

Severo's death coincided with the arrival of the photographer for whom the advertisement had been placed a few weeks earlier.

He was the first man to enter the village in a Model T Ford with black bodywork and headlights with electric bulbs. The car went as fast as a galloping horse and weighed as much as a whale's heart. The rumble of its four-cylinder petrol engine could be heard on the stone bridges, and the slow carts made way for its metal wheels to pass.

The photographer soon reached the house and parked on the driveway where Severo Bracamonte's accident had taken place a month earlier. The short brown-haired man got out of the car, jumping off the footboard wearing polished shoes with carved buttons.

His skin was the colour of ivory and two perfectly symmetrical cheeks emphasised his candid gaze. His grey hair was cut short and, though he was over forty, there was a brightness in his eyes that gave him an air of late youth.

Wearing a black veil, Serena came out onto the porch to welcome him. She congratulated him on his triumphant arrival.

'Look at the village children crowding around your car, Señor,' she remarked.

The photographer thanked her and introduced himself as Mateo San Mateo. Serena took this to be a borrowed name.

She invited him into the living room. He sat down in an armchair and, after carefully placing his jacket on top of a chest of drawers, clasped his hands in his lap. Glancing around the room, he took in the plumped chairs, the scent of chrysanthemums and the sheets hanging over the mirrors. He saw Serena's black veil, her puffy eyes and the wreaths of flowers and, despite knowing nothing of what had happened, offered his condolences. Caught off guard, she flushed.

With Severo's death still floating in the air, Mateo San Mateo trod carefully. He spoke of his reading and travels, of wives who lived comfortably without their husbands. The world was changing, he said, and women were born to build cities, create masterpieces and set up companies. They should be allowed to vote and be let into parliament. In the past, Gaulish women had been lawmakers and Huron women had taken part in councils of war.

'This century is lagging behind,' he smiled. 'You'll see – one day we'll have female presidents.'

Serena agreed. After a few simple exchanges, the photographer revealed himself to be more talkative than a shipwreck victim freshly fished out of the sea. He had an opinion on everything and expressed himself with rare distinction, punctuating his sentences with winks and knowing smiles.

He moved on to the topic of his profession. The boom in photography over recent years had opened up new possibilities, he said. He had specialised in photographing industrialists keen to embrace modernity, as well as in family portraits. Most of his clients were nouveau riche making up for their lack of illustrious ancestors with snaps of their naked babies.

'Kids love being photographed with violins they can't play,' San Mateo remarked.

Serena listened with interest. Despite the fact that he was younger than her, his mature understanding of the world made him seem older than he was.

He covered all kinds of subjects, using an Italianate Spanish to speak of political intrigue, various trends in the visual arts and the current fashions in clothing. All of this knowledge impressed her. Serena had heard on the radio that a revolution in colour photography had begun in Europe. Mateo San Mateo took up the subject with gusto, bemoaning the fact that the Atlantic took as long to cross as progress did to arrive.

Then came an endless stream of explanations of scientific techniques, darkrooms and developing baths.

'When the photo appears in the bath, it's like the birth of a child.'

Serena was enchanted with this. She liked everything about him – his voice, his gestures and the way he held himself. A captivating air of mystery burnt brightly in his eyes like a flame. There was no doubt about it, this was a man shaped by the luck or misfortune fate had thrown at him, a man full of original ideas, and she admired his intelligence, which stood out against the mediocrity of the times.

It was four in the afternoon. Ever the artist, San Mateo said he wished to make the most of the daylight and went to fetch his equipment from the car.

Serena was relieved. In all the years she had spent on the farm, this was the first man to have truly replied to an advertisement. The photographer came back carrying a tripod, a spotlight and a heavy camera which he struggled to hold under his arm. Everything was shiny, new and chrome-plated.

It took forever to set up the shot. He gave scholarly explanations about shutter speeds and exposures. He corrected Serena's posture, allowing himself to touch her waist.

'Now don't move,' he said.

Then he brought his face close to hers. He behaved with gentlemanly delicacy, placing his hand to her temple and gently tilting her head to one side.

Serena quivered, giddy with a rush of sensuality. She stood motionless, her head inclined, mouth half open and eyes raised. The hand touching her temple was as a compass to a ship lost in a storm.

The photographer said, 'Don't breathe.'

But the air had in any case ceased to enter Serena's lungs. Striking a fashionable pose, she stood in the bland surroundings of the living room before the camera, which was to capture a single image of this day.

Once the photograph had been taken, Serena joked, laughed and, for the space of an hour, rediscovered the joy she had lost so long ago. Then she suddenly remembered Eva Fuego and asked a servant to go and fetch her.

'My daughter won't be long,' she said.

But Eva Fuego, who had been called several times, was already standing stock-still in the doorway, just as Serena had done thirty years earlier, the day Severo had arrived.

She was staring scornfully at the photographer. Hatless, he sat on the arm of a chair, with a casual air about him, as if he owned the place.

Eva Fuego walked towards him, holding out her hand, and shook his firmly. San Mateo was taken aback.

'This gentleman is a photographer,' Serena told her, rosy-cheeked, all smiles. Then she added sweetly, as if already bracing herself for rejection, 'If you like, we could pose together?'

Eva Fuego was dressed in riding trousers, a tatty old shirt and a straw hat tilted over one ear. A tomboyish haircut accentuated her masculine side. Around her neck she wore a pendant in the shape of a rum-bottle stopper.

She turned towards the camera, tripod and spotlight, concluding that all of this equipment was taking up too much space in the living room. Sensing her hesitation, San Mateo did not wish to rush her.

'Let's see about that later,' he said.

It was getting dark and Serena asked him to stay for dinner. She asked her daughter to make a stew. Eva Fuego went out into the yard, entered the henhouse and caught a bird with ease, surprising the photographer.

He wished to make himself useful. Assuring them he had always helped women in the kitchen, he rolled up his sleeves and made a series of feminist remarks. Laughing and joking, they gathered about the stove.

He rounded off by saying, 'Luckily the world has changed.'

It was dark in the kitchen. By the wall, a feeble flame was licking the curved sides of the casserole, and a soft ray of light shone down from a bull's-eye window. At the back, a few hollow bulls' horns hung alongside some cabbage leaves and a large, cold mortar lay in the middle of the room like a sleeping monster.

San Mateo stood awaiting orders. Eva Fuego wrapped a blood-spattered apron covered in feathers around his waist. Staring directly at the photographer, she held the chicken tightly in her hands, made it swallow vinegar as she wrung its neck, then pricked it behind the ear with a sharp knife.

The bird writhed and struggled as it died, its blood dripping into the sink as its eyes glazed over. Then Eva Fuego plunged it into boiling water, closing its wings with one hand, plucked it and scorched its skin on a hotplate. Finally she cut off its feet at the joints and picked out its eyes with her fingers.

San Mateo was disgusted. In order to appear

composed, he asked, 'May I take a picture of you?'

Eva Fuego shrugged. San Mateo left the kitchen and Serena followed to help him carry in his equipment.

Holding the chicken in one hand, Eva Fuego used another small knife to make an incision at the bottom of its abdomen. She pulled out the gizzards and removed the lungs and guts, taking care not to pierce the bile sac.

She was about to throw the lot in the dustbin when a shiny object caught her attention. Amid the entrails, covered in blood, a stone was glistening. Startled, she picked it up and washed it thoroughly.

Holding it up to the light, Eva Fuego recognised what she was holding between her fingers as a nugget of gold, no bigger than a corn kernel, hidden in a hen's stomach.

She rummaged about in the kitchen, but found nothing. She moved plates, dirty pans and old tea towels. There was nothing but trails of blood, tufty head-feathers, bits of tongue and lumps of flesh. The nugget must have come from outside the house.

Eva Fuego looked out of the window towards the henhouse and began to wonder if the two hundred bright-orange-feathered birds inside it had been pecking at pirates' treasure for the past three centuries, and had Captain Henry Morgan's fortune hidden in their guts.

When San Mateo returned to take her portrait, Eva Fuego quickly hid the gold nugget in her apron pocket. Brimming with enthusiasm, the photographer gave a thorough explanation of the shot he planned to take. It would be a classic picture on a ten-centimetre plate, a portrait of a woman in which all the simplicity and nobility of the peasantry would be clear to see.

With more than a touch of self-indulgence, he remarked, 'Complicated men are fond of the simple things in life, isn't that so?'

He even assured her he would mount the photograph in a gold frame. Hearing the word 'gold', Eva Fuego shuddered. She silently clutched the nugget in her fist, and something powerful awoke inside her.

The next day, she got up before her mother and headed to the henhouse, certain of having located the treasure. The sun was slowly coming up. Frightened by her presence, the chickens ran out into the court-yard, noisily pecking at one another.

Eva Fuego inspected the floor, pulled up the boards and peered to look underneath them, but there was nothing there. She lifted the asphalt roof to check for a false ceiling. She ran her hands over the whole shed, the nesting boxes, the feeding and drinking troughs. As the henhouse was mounted on stilts, she lay down to look beneath it, but found only earth and blood raked up by the rain.

Then suddenly she discovered a hole in the chicken wire through which the hens seemed to be escaping. She followed the traces of footprints and feathers scattered across the ground. The marks continued all the way around the edge of the farm, running alongside an old fence and ending up at the doorway that led into the right-hand wing of the farm.

The space behind the house was not pleasant: it was obvious that only lizards and rats lived there. There was an opening in the wall and a smell of bird droppings and damp cellars. Eva Fuego knelt down to look inside.

It was the entrance to a tunnel with a narrow neck just wide enough to slip inside, which broadened out a dozen metres further on.

Eva Fuego snaked her way inside, flat on her stomach. She crawled cautiously through the dark passageway. She kept expecting to reach a dead end, but the tunnel went on further underground. Though the space was tight, dim and damp, she managed to keep going, pushing her body along with her elbows, the walls of the tunnel squeezing her shoulders.

Her heart began to race. Fear was taking hold of her. She continued along the stony, straw-covered ground amid the fetid stench of rotten eggs. From time to time her back scraped along the roof of the tunnel and she had to wiggle her pelvis to set herself free. She stopped and tried unsuccessfully to listen for the birds' squawking to gauge how far she had come.

All she could hear now was the light echo of her own breathing. The twists and turns of the underground passageway became ever tighter, coiling deeper like a black snake, and Eva Fuego was so afraid of the walls falling in that she stopped every metre to listen out for the slightest creaking of the earth.

She was overjoyed when she approached the end of the tunnel and glimpsed a shaft of grey light. A few metres further on, a gap opened up above her. She poked her head through, lifting herself up on her arms, and saw that the tunnel opened out into a gloomy, fully furnished room, which looked like a bedroom in the middle of a house.

She soon realised she was inside her own house, in the room the old lady shut herself up in every 1 November, and which they were forbidden to enter. The wallpaper was yellowed and the drapes destroyed by mites. Dry cigarettes had been left on a desk alongside a broken flask, a few candle stumps, a bottle of cinnamon wine and the key to a lock that no longer existed.

Eva Fuego noticed that some of the floorboards had been lifted, revealing a huge hole in the middle of the floor from which a mysterious light shone. Holding a lamp above the opening, she made out a jumble of antiques.

There, piled up in chests and leather bags, were hundreds of ducats, doubloons, louis, thalers, ciboria, monstrances, chalices and cloth of gold. Mother-of-pearl dishes, topaz diadems and cedar chests filled with carnelians, rubies and uncut stones, hundreds of Mexican crowns, swords and daggers, baldrics and roundel shields, and Roman army insignia all appeared before her eyes. The ground was strewn with rings and patens, candelabras, strings of bells and, in the middle, a metre-high gold statue with a breastplate weighing eight hundred pounds and a diamond-encrusted tunic.

All the continent's gold seemed to lie before her, from the Amazon to Ushuaia, from the slopes of the Andes to the coast of Brazil, from Araucanía to Venezuela. Like streams flowing into a great river, all the money from every port, the coins from every monastery, the taxes of every province, the worked gold of every fiefdom, the reserves of every bank and the purse of every prince seemed to converge here.

Eva Fuego sat on the ground, her hands trembling. She felt betrayed. Henry Morgan's treasure had always lain here, right under their feet, behind this little door, where the old woman had made fools of them for decades. She had learnt to make herself invisible, to become an anonymous passer-by, an intruder who went unnoticed.

Eva Fuego looked at all the gold in disbelief. She doubted she could ever find the words to describe it. Most of the objects were unfamiliar to her. She was amazed by the diameter of the crowns and the elaborate settings of the jewellery. She studied every detail of the arabesques on the candelabras and the sparkling cogs inside the clocks.

But of all the muddled thoughts colliding inside her head, she could not shake the memory of Severo Bracamonte. Faced with this dazzling sight, Eva Fuego could not bring herself to believe that this admirable and determined man had slept for thirty years above the treasure he had hunted all his life.

XIII

At the same time that Eva Fuego discovered the gold in the house, an oil deposit was discovered in the west of the country. It emerged like a Minotaur from the depths of its labyrinth and soon several companies sprang up to exploit it. It jolted the economy into action, migrants came pouring in, drilling began and the wealth generated soon ran into millions.

Engineers and scientists came from every corner of the country to drill and conduct tests. The old economy based on maize, cassava, cotton and tobacco was soon superseded by the oil industry. Exports surpassed those of coffee and cocoa. As more and more oil was extracted, it soon became the country's main source of revenue.

That same year, the first post office opened on the main square, painted red and white with a winged feather in bas-relief. A relay network was set up to make transport easier, allowing letters to arrive more quickly.

It was this post office that received the only two photographs the village was to see. The first was of Serena Bracamonte standing unsmiling in her living room, her hair pinned back in a half-ponytail, wearing a dress so rigid it seemed to be made of wood. The second was the portrait of Eva Fuego staring unblinkingly at the camera from behind the kitchen table, her hands stained with blood and feathers, with a dark, lonely look in her eyes. The photographs had been sent from the capital by Mateo San Mateo along with a note addressed to the two women, filled with endless polite expressions of sincere gratitude.

Serena examined the stamp, read the postmark and courteously sent back a thank-you letter, slipped inside a blue envelope.

A week later, San Mateo sent her a note to thank her for the thank-you letter, with a postcard depicting one of the main streets of the capital. In cramped handwriting on the back were the daringly familiar words 'Mi casa es tu casa'.

Serena sent a longer letter back, feigning interest in the shop signs in the picture, and taking the liberty of sharing some news of the farm.

This was how their correspondence began. She asked questions about city life and he replied with anecdotes and practical tips. They moved on from photography to discuss books, painting and music, and soon a constant flow of letters was passing between them, peppered with quotations from monks and famous writers.

Every letter was a joy to open. Serena received them in the greatest secrecy, going to fetch them from the post office herself and reading them discreetly on the way home.

The letters lifted her spirits, like a secret tribute. She looked forward to reading them as impatiently as she had once listened out for Esmeralda Cadenas's radio announcements.

San Mateo's handwriting was as fine and delicate as the man himself. He came from an old family documented by an Italian biographer and he counted many famous artists among his friends. His qualities were more apparent than his faults. He had a clarity of mind which made him free and a candour which made him happy, and Serena savoured his every word, her head tilted to one side, a smile on her lips, sitting by the flower pot underneath the tamarind tree.

Serena emerged from her bereavement more attractive and effervescent than ever, and this new burst of youthful freshness got the villagers talking. The circumstances of San Mateo's appearance had made her forget those of Severo's funeral.

She could sense a new existence, full of poetry and ambition, opening up in her middle years. Little by little she felt herself emerging from the anonymous isolation under which her passions had been buried, to seek enchantment and unveil her secrets with the quiet determination of a woman who has escaped her fate.

Around this time, Serena began wearing a little embroidered shawl over her shoulders and half-moon glasses for reading. One day she confessed in a letter that she had always been bored and went on to describe the dull business of her everyday life, complaining about the work of a distiller and all the tedious bookkeeping it entailed.

She wished she could live in a world without barrels and bottles in which she was free to tackle the great classical themes with nothing standing in the way of her happiness, a world in which she could hold back time, in which love was all.

From then on, love was as integral to their correspondence as ink. They returned to it again and again, using words like 'passion', 'feeling' and 'desire'.

She asked him if it was possible to love several people at once. San Mateo replied that this was sadly an undeniable talent of men. He tried to exclude himself from this assessment, avoiding both speaking about his past and compromising his future. And as Serena's eyes ran across the pages on which his own gaze had rested, she fell under the illusion that she understood this man without really knowing him.

She sank deeper into a world of revelations and intimate avowals. She admitted everything, her expectations and what wearied or worried her. San Mateo received this flood of confidences without judgement, but as something natural and necessary. His advice was noble, his responses thoughtful. He made the simplest things into absolute truths.

Serena began to dream of another wild, intrepid life of continents to explore and obstacles to overcome.

'You're a Quixote,' she wrote to him.

She wanted to know everything about him. She

wanted his intelligence to become so familiar to her that it would seem natural.

She kept looking back at herself a few years earlier, resigned to emptiness, sitting in her room pressing flowers for hours on end, and when the time came to harvest the sugar cane in February, everyone had to wait to fill the barrels, for that day she had read these words in a letter from San Mateo:

I would drink a barrel of rum if your heart was my reward.

It was like a revelation. Any remaining doubts evaporated. She seized a sheet of perfumed paper and, with a surge of spirit and resolve, bravely, audaciously ordered him back to the farm. She told him to come for her, to carry her away from her house, to wrest her from her very self.

She waited several days for San Mateo's reply and finally received a letter composed of just two words on yellow paper: 'Why me?'

She let a long time go by before replying with great assurance: 'Because only you could almost make my heart burst by brushing your hand against my temple.'

So San Mateo made his second trip to the farm. He arrived dressed in an alpaca-wool suit and gaiters, with silk gloves tucked under his armpit. He had put a little pink on his lips to bring out their colour. His beard was well groomed and a plaited white neckerchief protruded from his jacket; he smelt of talc.

When Serena heard the roar of the engine, the horn beeping and children playing around the car, she knew her life was about to change. It hit her as she went outside to meet him, rushing like a river, wearing a blue silk dress that accentuated her figure.

She had twisted her hair around a cherry sprig and at her neck she wore an elegant wax-flower necklace her mother had wrested from poverty. The habit of playing the grande dame had lent her an air of natural distinction and her skin had not suffered from thirty years of make-up. There was something of the Spanish duenna about her.

As soon as she saw San Mateo, Serena was certain she had made the right choice. She gazed around one last time at the patches of sugar cane on the hillsides, the caramel light running down towards the forest and the distant outline of the sugar mill.

She had grown up in this small corner of the valley, stifled by her surroundings. She needed to move, to fly away. It wasn't a whim, it was her right. No one had spent so long waiting for love as she, holed up in this isolated farm and never allowed to blossom.

And so she left the land of her childhood as if embracing a dream, escaping into exile. The determination in her eyes was so obvious that Eva Fuego didn't try to stop her.

For Eva Fuego, there was no heartache or sadness in saying goodbye. Rather, Serena's departure represented a kind of rebirth. Eva Fuego's destiny began where Serena's ended. All at once, she found herself revelling in the prospect of being left alone, in the certainty of being able to devote herself to her secret passion.

Eva Fuego could still see the hole in the middle of the room, the lifted floorboards and the treasure left there gathering dust, returned to the shadows.

'You'll write to me, won't you?' asked Serena, her face covered in tears.

Eva Fuego smiled. She was as closed and silent as the treasure chest itself. While her mother clasped her in her arms and heaped sweet words upon her, she was trying to work out how much her gold was worth.

She began drawing up plans for new hiding places. Anything that could withstand humidity – the precious stones, ornaments and jewellery – could be buried on the riverbanks, ten feet underground, too deep to detect. As for the objects which could not go near water – the fabrics, papers and silks – those should be deposited in dry land, in narrow crevasses. She would draw up a register of every last ciborium, every pearl and every jewel. She would list all the different currencies, the relative sparkle of each stone, and would sort true gold from fool's using a bottle of aqua regia.

Serena cried, sobbed, made all kinds of promises, while Eva Fuego told herself that since the door to the treasure room creaked, she would have to silence it with a drop of oil.

Serena looked her straight in the eye.

'Now you're the woman of the house.'

Eva Fuego wanted to tell her she was now the woman of the entire world. She secretly knew she would make men her subjects, the village her kingdom. She would have the power that comes of excess, a taste for the impossible and chasing feverish horizons, and an inner voice would whisper the words of queens in her ear.

That day, as Serena left, Eva Fuego, without ancestor or heir, joined the race of wild animals who know no limits, who, in waging war against themselves, live several lives in one existence.

XIV

After Severo Bracamonte's death and Serena's departure, Eva Fuego took over the running of the farm, carrying on the now booming business her parents had founded. Like pirates investing the spoils of their pillage in property on dry land, she ploughed her treasure into the family plantation and expanded the company, which would be held up as an example for many years to come.

First she fenced off the hectares of sugar cane to create a border around the property. Soon the crops spread as far as the opposite bank of the river where, much to everyone's surprise, she had bought new plots of land.

Everybody imagined the money must have come from her inheritance. No one suspected that every night Eva Fuego slowly opened her eyes, went down to the living room, lantern in hand, and made her way to the back room. She had changed the lock and carried its heavy key around her neck. Before opening the door, she looked around her carefully to ensure she was quite alone, and soundlessly turned the key.

Inside the room, Eva Fuego felt a kind of thrill when she peered into the hole and plunged her hands into her riches, filling bags with treasure with avaricious glee as short strands of hair fell over the scar on her temple.

A column still was imported from Europe to replace the old stills. This piece of modern machinery arrived complete with two enormous cylinders to facilitate the fermentation of the molasses. The steam turned the mills. A little train was brought in to transport the canes, and the time saved overall led to an improvement in the quality of the spirits.

On the farm, Eva Fuego constructed terraces, put in rows of palm trees and built up the reserves. She delegated nothing and oversaw everything, running the workshops, supervising the filtering process and advising on building works. She was everywhere at once.

She had a bridge constructed over the river and conducted the opening ceremony herself. The swamps were drained, the roads paved and the riverbanks raised. The rapidly expanding business provided a living for two hundred workers and called upon the services of at least fifty artisan coopers and thirty oarsmen.

The number of oxen, cows and sheep all increased. The crops yielded good harvests and the livestock were sold at a healthy profit. She was the only woman in the region to talk of 'square hours', meaning the time it took to ride across a plot of land. The authorities assigned her land stretching as far as the eye could see.

Barns, grain stores and furrowed fields sprang up on all sides. Dozens of woodcutters were taken on to stock the mills and run the sawmill. Cane cutters attracted by the booming business came flooding in from neighbouring villages, ready to work day and night for the chance to double their pay.

In order to curry favour, Eva Fuego financed a number of municipal works. She employed a landscape gardener to transform a patch on the edge of the forest where there had been nothing but shacks and marshes. He designed an English-style garden with sweeping curves, planted with different varieties of trees and surrounded by a circle of hazel bushes.

She had a half-timbered pavilion built with beaten-earth walls to put on shows performed by the workers. At the end of a long day, an audience of woodcutters and gleaners flocked to the new venue to watch Florentino duelling with the Devil.

In order to show her respect for traditional beliefs, she poured a barrel of rum on the ground, appealing to the spirits of the Santería, then organised processions in honour of St Benedict and St Expeditus, the first of whom was black, the second not recognised by the Church.

In order to please the Catholics, she paid for the ground around the chapels to be cleared and the graves restored. She even offered them a bronze bell cast from cannon used in the battle for Independence.

She had the river dredged, diverting part of it to build a lock and water mill and generate her own energy. The barrels of rum were rolled down to vans which shuttled between the farm and a little harbour from where they were taken to the buyers' warehouses in pirogues.

Since Eva Fuego produced high-quality rum at a good price, she soon became the region's premier restaurant supplier. Almost every bottle on every table came from her distillery.

But the competition between different brands was becoming fierce. The labels needed to be more eye-catching in order to attract consumers.

She organised a competition for the best graphic artists and illustrators in the region. Labels landed on her table with pictures of raging seas, a bare-breasted Creole woman or the profile of Admiral Nelson, but the one which caught her attention was a small grey etching, without embellishments or palm trees, on which Captain Henry Morgan stood with his leg resting on an overturned barrel with a bottle in his hand.

The print run for the labels was huge. Eva Fuego added the name of her business and the attribute 'old rum'. She put advertisements everywhere and had branded ashtrays, tiles, knives, key rings, games and posters made.

She met people working at every stage of the rum-making process, from cutting the canes to illustrating the bottoms of glasses. She gave strict orders, would not tolerate misconduct, seldom smiled, never apologised, and one sensed in this remote woman all the characteristics typical of those destined to make a fortune.

She lost her femininity, wearing only wellington boots, worn gloves and a frayed scarf with twisted ends. She had a little leather pouch attached to her belt in which she claimed to store gunpowder, but everyone knew it was where she kept her gold.

Her face had hardened, her features tightened, and now the burn on her temple was beginning to eat into her left eyebrow. She was built of tight nerves, swollen arteries and stitched leather. She never wore perfume, naturally exuding the earthy aroma of the fields.

At church or in the village square, people would greet her with a fearful smile, keeping their distance. She had such a severe look about her you would almost think she was preparing a coup d'état in her own village. People spoke of her as a supreme being and, as with idols, rumour disguised her features under a veil of hearsay.

One night a group of bandits broke into the storehouses, put gunpowder in the barrels and set them alight. They were acting on the orders of a certain John Kinloch, a British landowner and proprietor of a rum distillery who had devised this tactic as a means of increasing his market share.

Eva Fuego secretly took a decision. Though she knew how effective firearms could be, she feared opening the way to local warfare, popular uprisings and riots that would be difficult to subdue. A few days later, John Kinloch quietly disappeared. His body would be found only ten years later, perfectly preserved in alcohol inside an old barrel in Eva Fuego's cellar.

She became something of a legend and no longer went out unescorted. She built a new three-foot-thick wall around the main house. A sentry box protected the entrance and two giants from the islands were put on surveillance duty, continually patrolling the grounds at night. The watchmen assigned to the warehouses were told to shoot at any passing shadow; security guards did their rounds with dogs, and the peasants were made to wear a uniform of a blue shirt and trousers with yellow piping.

Soon she began to rely on imports. She was criticised for buying in tools and seeds from abroad, turning her nose up at local products. She had cheese sent from Savoy, Tabasco from Mexico, prunes from Agen and wine from Bordeaux.

Vans loaded and unloaded cases of goods on a daily basis. Frogs' legs, Burgundy snails and York hams were served at her table every night alongside canned food from Miami which always had the same metallic taste, whether the contents were asparagus or peas.

Rum production reached such a peak that her crop was no longer sufficient. Molasses had to be bought in from neighbouring planters to meet the needs of the distillery. Eva Fuego went around by car, leaving her house in the care of a few faithful servants. It was said that she could keep an eye on her workers from a distance simply by reading the ripples on the surface of a vase of water.

But while everyone thought she was far away pursuing her business ventures, Eva Fuego spent most of her time in the room that was out of bounds, sitting in the dark, counting her gold. She could be found there at any time of day, her hands thrust into leather sacks filled to bursting with sparkling gems, trying to work out just how much wealth she had to distribute among her own burning ambitions.

At night, she found herself sitting alone in a wing chair on the terrace with a hundred coins tucked under her dress, as if she were the lookout on a ship adrift in the middle of the sea. She remained there until late at night, looking out past the balustrade at the dark fields and the slow black flow of the river where children were feeding a sad-looking parrot, their feet dabbling in oil. She seemed to be waiting for destiny to present her with some marvel, though exactly what, she did not know.

So she would go upstairs to bed, looking out at the shafts of moonlight across the garden, breathing in the pure, dark air, safe in the knowledge she would be sleeping with one hundred kilos of gold hidden between her legs.

At her peak, she was stronger and more elusive than ever. No one ever contradicted her. She made quick calculations, kept her word and was well practised at greasing palms. She cultivated useful contacts and pursued bad payers.

She was never seen to wear a ring on her finger, though she never held out her hand to be kissed. She had no wish to marry, and looked upon domestic chores with disdain. A ring around her finger seemed to her akin to a chain around her neck. She was a free agent, faithful only to freedom itself.

Eva Fuego already had seven distillery rooms and more than four hundred workers when war broke out in a neighbouring country. At the front, alcohol was mixed with cotton and ether to make gunpowder.

The bloodier the war became, the more Eva Fuego's business flourished. Rum was needed to disinfect wounds, anaesthetise amputees and raise morale among the troops before assaults.

She was considered a criminal, a profiteer, accused of being a parasite feeding off foreign conflicts. But despite her controversial reputation, the prosperity of her factory attracted others and soon the region was filled with merchants, livestock farmers and manufacturers. Here and there she created new businesses where she saw the chance of a profit.

Soon she had doubled her client base and was able to set up a sugar refinery. She even planned to launch a chain of bars, create a heritage office, build canal locks and paths, things which, during that century of excess in the Caribbean, could all be brought about in just a decade, creating one of those extraordinary landscapes only seen in the tropics.

XV

Talk of Eva Fuego's success revived interest in Henry Morgan's treasure. Thanks to her, men came to set up makeshift camps beside the river. Wading in water up to their knees, they took the area by storm, using a big pump to wash gravel, and probe and sift the silt of the river. Short of means, they desperately sought funds to finance their expeditions.

It was a simple deal: information in exchange for money. The cleverest among them knocked at the doors of the local bourgeois, telling tall tales to arouse their spirit of adventure. Others came across charitable souls who believed in legends and were willing to stake their fortunes on dangerous expeditions.

Eva Fuego saw the chance to benefit from the situation. She set up a company with twenty thousand 10-peso shares for sale, in order to attract the highest possible number of signatories and gather all the existing information on the treasures of the region.

She held meetings with representatives of various associations, visited specialists and made use of Severo Bracamonte's maps. She let it be known that an aristocratic lady had once raised enormous funds for an expedition whose backers had made twenty times their initial investment when a Spanish galleon had been discovered with its hold stuffed with gold.

A month later, the Company of Treasure Hunters was established to finance prospecting in the area. A procession of cars rolled into the village one 1 November.

Twenty men and four families got out amid a huge cloud of dust. They spoke by turns in English, German, Spanish and French. Eva Fuego was waiting for them outside the house, the expression on her face unreadable.

As indifferently as Serena Otero had watched a young, bold and proud Severo approaching the farm through the guava trees thirty years earlier, and as suspiciously as Severo Bracamonte had eyed the Andalusian riding up on horseback some years later, so the rich, respected Eva Fuego now stood looking down from the top of her steps as this intrepid company came marching towards her.

The company's arrival sent shock waves through the village. The newcomers had prefabricated buildings and kept their provisions in refrigerators. They had an electricity generator to power portable radios, walkie-talkies and metal detectors.

A fat, talkative millionaire from Kansas hoping to realise an adolescent dream had provided five pneumatic drills and a powerful compressor. There was also an old couple, whose faces were full of wrinkles and whose arms were covered in gnarled veins, and who spoke with a strong German accent; several northern Frenchmen in leather jackets with washed-out, almost greyish skin, and blue tattoos on their chests; some girls, come to enjoy themselves and get rich, who never stopped laughing; male and female scientists and measurement-takers, and even a film director who wanted to make a documentary and have exclusive rights over all the images of the expedition.

They agreed on the area of land to be prospected. It spanned a hundred hectares and, strangely, fell within the boundaries of Eva Fuego's property. The old drawings and pirates' maps were no longer necessary: the company put its trust in specialists who drilled out samples of earth and examined them under electron microscopes.

A few dozen metres from the house, this little world grew quickly. The hillsides bristled with wires, wooden posts and coloured flags.

First the land was levelled in order to bring in the detection equipment. As soon as the needle began to swing, men would frantically begin digging. There was a fun, celebratory atmosphere. The millionaire had himself filmed digging, and the girls in their skirts fell about laughing.

One day, the needle shook so violently that everyone rushed to pick up a shovel in order to be the first to uncover the treasure chest. But all they found was a biscuit tin and a golden pellet from a hunting rifle.

Around the table in the evenings, the members of the company told thousands of stories of buccaneers. These were slipper-wearing gold-diggers, readers of pirate stories who had never truly searched for treasure.

The loud German pompously stated that no one had yet found the galleon of the Invincible Armada buried in Tobermory Bay, a wreck estimated to be worth thirty million ducats. A small, sharp-eyed Frenchman spoke of the treasures aboard the *San José*, sunk by the British in 1708 off the coast of Cartagena.

The Kansas millionaire drew on a cigar and talked in a nasal twang of the Silver Fleet at the bottom of Vigo harbour, in San Simon Bay, close to the land of Ophir. Two girls who might have been sisters continually interrupted one another as they gave an account of how on Île Bourbon, specifically the plain of Butor, tons of gold had been unearthed not far from Sainte-Clotilde Church.

When they got onto the topic of the legend of Henry Morgan, everyone let out a sigh, and some turned to look dreamily out at the surrounding countryside, their minds filled with thoughts of seafarers.

Eva Fuego listened without saying a word. Her face betrayed no emotion, but her heart was filled with deceit. She alone knew the exact location of the treasure which the company had cloaked in legend. She alone knew the truth, while taking a perverse pleasure in encouraging everyone at the end of the meal to persevere with their search the next day.

Then she would go home, lock the door behind her and slip inside the back room, pale-faced, stooping, her dull, disaffected eyes staring into the glow of her gold amid the whisperings of her vanity.

After a month, tongues were wagging in the village over the amount the company had spent. Questions were asked about where Eva Fuego's money had come from and how clean her business was.

In order to fend off accusations, she financed the first tramline, which ran down the main street. Meanwhile the first clock was put up on the pediment of the town hall, so that time should be the preserve of no man.

Eva Fuego was even cynical enough to have a bronze plate engraved with the message that should any treasure be discovered, it was to be shared among all the inhabitants of the village.

The members of the company began to show their impatience. They demanded more detailed drawings, more precise maps, and even went as far as to question the existence of the treasure. Eva Fuego protested.

Lawyers were called in. Part of the company wanted to withdraw its stake, demanding a refund, but the shareholders quickly discovered they had signed their money over to a non-existent frontman, whose name did not appear on any documents.

Ruined, the Kansas millionaire took Eva Fuego to court. The plaintiffs ruthlessly pursued the woman who had shown them no pity. But Eva Fuego spent a fortune buying off judges and, after lengthy proceedings, and without signing a single document,

Eva Fuego had the case against her dropped.

At the age of thirty-five, the orphan girl who had been found in the woods cloaked in ashes and the scent of death had risen to the rank of queen.

It occurred to her to throw a lavish party as a means of flaunting the extent of her power. Her resounding success in the courts had made her hungry for more. She told herself a party would be a good way of maintaining her influence over judges and elected officials, attracting foreign investors and winning over the rich producers of 'old rums', who still had the monopoly on the Caribbean. She soon forgot the business with the Company of Treasure Hunters and, at the height of her fame, set a date for the party.

XVI

XVI

The party was among the most talked about of its day, setting both pens and drinks flowing. The house was decked out in bridal white.

In preparation for the big event, streams of traders came, offering goods for sale, followed by pedlars pushing trolleys of local curiosities and novelties from Europe.

Eva Fuego spent whatever was necessary to have the farm decorated with kilometres of garlands, streamers and ribbons. An actor offered his services to come dressed as Captain Henry Morgan with a sabre in his belt and a pistol in hand and mingle with the party guests.

Finally an Asian merchant stepped forward, lifted the tarpaulin off his load and showed Eva Fuego his collection of powder bombs, which were famed throughout the continent.

'The choice is yours, Señora. We've got flame-throwers, cascades, fountains and rockets in every colour.'

Eva Fuego had heard of these fireworks from China which made nitrate flowers blossom in the sky. Booming like thunder, the explosives lent those who used them a certain prestige.

She saw the fireworks as a symbol of her stature, the absolute confirmation of her authority, and bought entire boxes to be stashed away in the store where the barrels were aged.

The party began in the afternoon. In honour of the distillery, a stone pool with three pink marble fountains had been placed at the front of the house into which five hundred bottles of rum, four hundred bottles of Malaga wine, ten litres of water, three hundred kilos of sugar and two hundred nutmegs had been poured. A thousand lemons had been pressed and stirred by children for two days to serve almost four hundred guests.

The country's top master rum-maker organised tasting sessions. He demonstrated how to make blends, mix alcohols and create cocktails, and served shrubs, alexandras, cachaças and daiquiris. He claimed that the secret to making the best cocktails was to hold a glass of citrus fruit beside a bottle of rum as a ray of sunlight shone through it.

Pineapple-flavoured marinades were prepared to go with seafood. Amber spirits gave a kick to spiced saddle of rabbit and crayfish tails. White rum was flambéed over bananas, papayas and desserts of every kind. The butter had been sculpted into the shape of a bottle.

The party was so crowded that people had to push their way through. An endless stream of the illustrious and influential mingled together: diplomats, artists, planters and scientists. Servants weaved in and out of the crowd holding earthenware pots bristling with cigars and doling out sugar.

One course followed another, and bowls brimming with Swiss chocolate and Lebanese pastries were passed round. The scent of violet drops wafted from silver trays on which swan and foie gras were served with absinthe. A bare-chested black athlete offered triangles of fruit off the tip of a Spanish dagger.

Oysters and octopus had been brought in from Mochima. The tables were laden with jugs of crushed ice and rum babas. A chandelier had been hung up and swords taken out of their sheepskin sheaths and placed on pedestal tables, gleaming as if being displayed for sale, their handles decorated with Latin inscriptions.

Porcelain plates holding live crabs and confit quail were handed round. Larks were served by weight, rather than individually. Ortolan breasts, swallow nests and blue toucan meat, apparently a delicacy of Trinidad and Tobago, were presented on beds of salad.

There was a tam-tam concert and African dancing. Oboes and cymbals were brought in on gypsy caravans, and a harp was even dragged in on an oxcart. Dozens of violinists were dotted about among the plantations. Beside the henhouse, a brass band played country tunes no one recognised.

Suddenly the music stopped, a trumpet blared like a thunderbolt, a curtain opened and Eva Fuego appeared on the front steps, dressed as Diana the huntress in all her glory.

The torches surrounding her gave her skin a bronze glow and turned her scar a deeper vermilion red. Her gold-dusted hair undulated over her broad shoulders. A ruby was set in the V of her sea-silk dress, adorned with mother-of-pearl shells. In her hand she held a wooden cane made to resemble the nodes and internodes of sugar cane, with a sculpted emerald handle.

Eva Fuego entered the crowd, greeting her guests with carefully dotted about gestures, giving strong and haughty stares like a puma surveying lowly farm animals.

Here there was talk of methods for ageing alcohol and agricultural techniques. There, high-ranking military officers, weighed down with decorations, and with their swords permanently slung across their bodies, recounted their war experiences.

It was an odd and rowdy bunch, half local, half foreign, frequenters of private clubs, smoking rooms and gaming tables. The hubbub grew louder, figures coming and going like shadows. They watched one another, studied one another; the crowd had a thousand eyes.

Eva Fuego went from group to group. She reigned over her domain, fulfilling every need, counting bottles, asking the waiters questions. Hookah pipes passed from hand to hand, filling the air with scented smoke. In the middle, a peacock with a gilded beak strutted among the guests, fanning its feathers.

At midnight, two consuls arrived on hooded mares.

They brought with them a couple of caged macaws and a zebra transported in a ship's hold, which knelt before Eva Fuego on a bed of orchids.

A celebration such as this had not been seen since the times of the Borgias. A theatre troupe composed a ballad about it which was still being sung at fairs thirty years later.

As the party reached its peak, Eva Fuego sent a boy down to the store where the barrels of rum languished, to bring out the fireworks.

The casks were stacked up along the four walls, reaching as high as the ceiling. The boy entered the room holding a rudimentary candle which gave off more smoke than light. It was covered in salt and oil.

He stumbled about as he looked for the box of fireworks and, suffering from the effects of both alcohol and candle smoke, he let a spark fall onto the liquid that had trickled out of a barrel.

A flame suddenly flared up. Frightened, the boy let go of the candle. The spilt rum, the dry straw, the wooden barrels, the gunpowder inside the rockets – all of it caught fire alarmingly quickly.

'Fire! Fire!'

Hearing this word, Eva Fuego felt the burn on her face redden. Panic spread through the crowd. A cloud of smoke billowed down the hill and, in the distance, the first flames sent fear into the hearts of the children.

On the farm, people were shouting and shoving. Something exploded in the storehouse. The banging and thudding sent everyone running towards the exit.

Eva Fuego headed towards the store as smoke poured from all sides. The flames were creeping through the wall panels, mounting an attack on the sky, and the wood crackled, crunched and began to split. Eva Fuego choked on the scorching air as terrified people ran past her.

One by one the barrels began to explode, thousands of litres of alcohol going up in flames, splinters of wood flying into the air, and the fireworks set off an enormous blaze.

Eva Fuego ordered the bravest men to come to the storehouse, open the river lock and fill buckets of water. Thirty men joined together to form a human chain. They went up and down tall ladders, disappearing into swirls of thick black smoke and coming out again coughing, spitting and vomiting.

When it became clear that the fire was not being extinguished, Eva Fuego flew into a rage. The year's output, which represented the bulk of her investment, must be saved at all costs.

She had an idea. The barrels could be cut loose and rolled down towards the river. Whipped up by the wind, the fire swelled like the sea. The mountain of gunpowder was setting bombs off in every direction, exploding in neighbouring farms and frightening the animals.

No one dared go near the storehouse now. Eva Fuego made for the burning building herself, lifting her dress and striding fearlessly onwards.

They saw her enter the thick smoke and disappear.

But the flames pushed her back, her dress caught light, and what they saw coming out was not barrels rolling down to the river, but the figure of Eva Fuego suddenly rushing from the storehouse like a human torch, letting out appalling screams, running towards the river to throw herself into the water as fireworks exploded in the sky.

She fell into the water. The current was strong and the rapids quickly carried her away. Men hurried along the riverbanks to try to catch her, but they could not find her.

They had been looking for several minutes when suddenly Eva Fuego's body came to the surface two or three times, like a piece of driftwood bobbing between the stones.

They shouted from the banks. Oarsmen were called urgently and riders set off on horseback to follow the river, scouring the banks. Within the hour, the whole region had heard the news of Eva Fuego's disappearance.

Everyone had their own version of events. Journalists were sent in to investigate. Soon a crowd of curious onlookers had gathered in front of the house.

At daybreak, Eva Fuego's body had still not been fished out of the river. The police organised searches downstream and in the surrounding woods. A dozen detectives were called in and pools and septic tanks were drained.

The light and laughter of the party was hushed

by a silent dawn. Men took apart what was left of the storehouse. Burst barrels, charred beams and the remnants of the building's frame were thrown away. And all that remained of Eva Fuego was a pile of smouldering ashes and a ruined, solitary farm which three generations of women had abandoned.

XVII

The fire at the party left a pall of ash hanging in the sky that took three years, ten months and five days to clear.

It stopped the sun from shining and the rain from falling. Eventually the ash began consuming the earth. The once verdant valley, damp along the banks of the river, rich in humus and mineral salts, sheltered by forests and dense vegetation, now looked like a savannah. Erosion had made the razed ground barren. The fire had wiped out plant life, killed as yet unhatched birds and left burrows empty.

Pond water turned green. Crumbling rocks appeared like old castles in the landscape. The mills stopped turning. The workshops and presses ground to a halt. The dry climate sped up evaporation, so that when the barrels were opened, they were found to be empty.

Old molasses rotted in the vats. On the plantations, the undergrowth became thick, the bushes dense with thorn and the canes tall. Thus half a century after Severo Bracamonte's arrival, the vast, once flourishing area he had developed, now withered under a black patch of sky, and the ash carried on the wind in the midst of this national disaster, dusted everything around with black gold.

Houses, farms and other dwellings were coated grey. Bells had had to be hung round the necks of the oxen because they kicked up so much dust they could not be seen on the road. The air was so polluted that the pale-faced children had a bitter taste in their mouths, never stopped coughing and were made to wear masks.

The smell of the fire had infiltrated the air and millions of grey snowflakes fell on canaries' cages, babies' cribs and horses in their stables. People looked up at the sky and saw only a blanket of cloud and smog falling on tarpaulin roofs and window panes.

'The country is burning,' they would say.

Eva Fuego's disappearance turned everything upside down. The village had come to depend on the business she brought in, and her neighbours now began to see the downsides of the monopoly she held.

When Eva Fuego had suddenly come into money, the distillery had boomed and the business had become the pride of the region. But a side effect had been to encourage idleness and neglect. So much was now imported that no one bothered to cultivate their own fields. Coffee, cocoa, maize and cotton ran short, despite this being the only place able to produce them.

The prosperity of the Bracamonte farm had been both the making and the undoing of the village. There was something of a biblical curse about it.

Holding Eva Fuego responsible for everything that had happened, the villagers looted her property. They pulled apart furniture, cleaned out her living room and ransacked the bedrooms, stable and attic.

They forced open the door to the cellar where they found a few barrels still containing rum. They used axes to get into them and taste what was inside.

'That's Eva Fuego's rum,' one of them pointed out. 'It'll bring bad luck.'

Nonetheless the casks were opened and for several months they drank to their hearts' content. When the barrels ran dry, they were cut in half to make flower containers, which is how they discovered the corpse of John Kinloch, the English rum-maker, rolled up in a ball, naked, the only man who had ever tried to attack Eva Fuego, preserved in alcohol for the past ten years.

It was around this time that Serena was seen in the village again.

She claimed never to have heard the news of Eva Fuego's death. Her return was the result of a different kind of pain; she was consumed by a different kind of suffering. She arrived carrying a secret wound which, by the dead look behind her eyes, appeared to have crushed her.

She had eventually tired of Mateo San Mateo, as she had of every man before him. So enthusiastically rebellious, so sure of her feelings had she been when she had left, that she returned devastated, her soul ripped from her.

Muslin headdresses hid the wrinkles appearing on her pale brow. Trials of the heart and dashed hopes had made her face harden and yellow like an old book, and around her neck she wore a string of pearls which had lost their lustre. She had kept the blue silk dress that had made her the talk of the town in her youth, and which she was now too old to wear. Sadness gave back what time had taken away.

As she arrived in the main square, Serena's heart was heavy. Here she was again in this arid land, whose every detail was familiar to her.

She recognised the lonely, oppressive horizon she had stared into on so many bored evenings. Once again she could smell the rising scent of ploughed land which had suffocated her since birth, like the damp walls of a convent. In the distance she made out the church steeple piercing the faded sky beside the cemetery where her mother and father lay side by side beneath two aloes. She saw the untended garden where Severo had been cremated, where nothing now stood but a low sandy wall.

A hundred bitter hopes, a hundred quiet yearnings, a hundred silent prayers came back to her. The deep, dull, dry past she had been so thrilled to leave behind was now resurfacing again as if it had never left her.

She walked the streets unhurriedly towards her house. The wreck of the farm looked like a medieval ruin. The stone had turned grey, dark green in places where it was choked with ivy.

The path of guava trees leading up to the three front steps was overgrown with brambles and was now nothing but a narrow and flowerless track.

Serena stepped over the bracken to reach the front of the house. The balustrades had gone brown, licked by the flames, and the gate, barred with planks of wood, had rusted shut. Nettles and weeds were growing in the white gravel and the seeds of parasitic plants carried on the wind had sprouted here and there on the steps. It was as if no one had ever crossed this lonely veranda, which nature had reclaimed as its own.

In the centre, the Diana statue stood on its green-tinged pedestal, damaged around the edges. Centuries of lying neglected in the damp ground had weathered the marble, like skin tanned by the sun. She had been moved from earth to sun, from sun to smog, and these displacements had given her a sad air of dignity.

The marks on her body, her eroded features, deep wrinkles and pockmarked face offered her a second chance at beauty, a second renaissance, delicately veiled in ash. Like Serena, she had endured the ravages of time, weariness and tragedy in her own way.

Serena opened the front door and went inside. The ground was strewn with debris. Swallows had made their nests in the corners of the windows and lizards slid through cracks in the ceiling. Every step on the staircase creaked; every bedroom had been stripped bare.

The main room which had once been the dining area was cold and empty, and streaks of mould ran across the two photographs of Serena and Eva Fuego that still hung on the wall.

As she walked on, Serena was surprised to see the door to the back room hanging open, where it had always been locked. She could almost see the little old woman dragging her woe through the house every 1 November, empty bucket in hand, leaving the scent of cinnamon in her wake.

And so, to satisfy a lifelong curiosity, she entered the forbidden room for the very first time.

It led into a dark bedroom that smelt of stale ashes. Moisture had left blisters in the wallpaper and the doorway was blocked by upturned furniture.

As her eyes slowly adjusted to the gloom, Serena saw an old, ugly, broken-windowed room which was larger than it first appeared. The floor creaked beneath her feet. It looked as if an axe had been taken to it to lift the boards, and a few rusty nails seemed to be all that was holding it together. It must once have been a bright and airy room, but was now so faded, dreary and unkempt it made Serena shiver.

She was about to close the door when she saw a movement under a woollen blanket from which a purplish-red foot the size of a puppy's paw was sticking out.

When Serena pulled the cover back, she saw the curled-up body of an animal that was barely breathing. Its head was bare and darker than bronze. Its nose was made up of two holes in the middle of its face. Its cheeks were blackened in places and furrowed like a ploughed field.

The animal turned towards Serena. Two empty eyes stared at her, and she cried out in horror. She stepped back, bringing her hands to her mouth. Lying on the floor, muscles flayed, burnt to her very soul, was Eva Fuego.

Her daughter had survived for years living under this blanket in the dust like an injured beast. She writhed about, gasping in pain, her breath foul. The tattered clothes covering her shoulders revealed glimpses of waxen, charred skin, swollen with scales. Scraps of flesh hung off the withered body she could no longer lift.

As she recognised her mother, Eva Fuego let out a piercing cry, but no other sound came from her throat. She moved painfully, pushing back the cover to reveal her bare legs.

The room was lit with a yellow glow and there between the pulled-up floorboards appeared a carpet sprinkled with a thousand jewels, ornate pieces of lace, silver, silk brocade, fine china and sacks of gold coins.

The creature had slept for three years upon a bed of emeralds, rubies of every size, silks and gems, inside this alcove, drinking in the light of her treasure. Nothing could be sadder than this prisoner chained to herself, surviving in this crumbling corner, licking her gold as if it were a wound.

Serena was rooted to the spot. A memory suddenly came back to her of the pure child with the rusty-red coat, born out of a burnt plantation. She saw once more her daughter's tiny heaving chest, round head and fearful eyes.

All at once Serena's maternal instincts returned. She scoured the room, searching through drawers, shelves and cupboards. Inside a dresser she found some plants, cinnamon wine and candles.

With slow, precise movements, she knelt beside Eva Fuego and, with the same reverent care she had shown her daughter since the girl's childhood, applied compresses over various parts of her body to enable the burns to heal.

Her skin was like crumpled paper, as thin as onion skin and fragile as velvet, and her wounds reopened every time she moved. But when Serena applied her dressings, Eva Fuego stopped moaning. She simply stared at her mother with absent eyes.

This tough, tyrannical body, which for thirty years had inspired so much fear, had shrivelled to become a frail and defenceless thing. She looked like the captain dying aboard his wrecked ship in the middle of the Caribbean, with only enough strength to clutch his treasure in his arms.

That night, Eva Fuego died amid the scent of almond trees. A silent sorrow ran through Serena's heart. She mourned her daughter's downfall, the end of a defeated existence.

Sitting on the floor beside the corpse, once the bearer of such riches and now so poor, she felt she had nothing left. She decided to put the farm up for sale for a ridiculously low price. In the deeds to the property, a clause stipulated that the new owners must agree to leave the room at the back untouched.

And so Serena left the farm, closing the door behind her and turning the key several times, knowing already that she would be back every 1 November wearing a lace dress and carrying an empty bucket, to mourn her daughter and her two husbands. For all that remained of her lost lineage, of her life's black sugar, was Henry Morgan's treasure, which she had never tried to find.